The Complete Sonoma Summers Series

Never Say Never
Never Say No To Love
Never Say Goodbye

Jesse Devyn Crowe

PHOENIX PUBLICATIONS
ARDENVOIR, WA

Sonoma Summers Series © 2020 Jesse Devyn Crowe and Phoenix Publications, Ardenvoir, Washington.

Never Say Never © 2019 Jesse Devyn Crowe and Phoenix Publications, Ardenvoir, Washington, Never Say No To Love © 2019 Jesse Devyn Crowe and Phoenix Publications, Ardenvoir, Washington, Never Say Goodbye © 2019 Jesse Devyn Crowe and Phoenix Publications, Ardenvoir, Washington

Cover Images: Adobe Stock ©elnariz and © Bjorn Bakstad, © deagreez and © Diego © santypan, © Jeffrey Schwartz

ISBN: 0-9787954-8-2

CONTENTS

Never Say Never

Sonoma Summers Series (Book 1)

Jesse Devyn Crowe

PHOENIX PUBLICATIONS
ARDENVOIR, WA

*In recognition of the endless wheel of births and deaths,
and the love shared along the way...*

Chapter One

When I first met Jay Green I thought he was an absolute ass. An arrogant, red-neck, chauvinistic ass, no less, whose Texas accent offended my liberal California ears. My boss, the amply-bearded Earl Wyse, Sonoma Diesel's Service Manager, introduced us on a Monday morning, the two men leaning their bony elbows on my clean Formica counter in the front lobby and sipping coffee out of cups that probably hadn't been washed since the New York Jets won the Super Bowl.

Not that I cared about what bacterium colonies were shacking up in those stained coffee cups, it was more that the guys were oblivious to the scrunge — either that or they simply didn't do dishes and expected me to do them. Since I wasn't a maid or a waitress (anymore), I pretty much avoided any tasks that reeked too much of female servitude, which meant I didn't do dishes either and left the dirty coffee cups for people to clean up after themselves. Except no one ever did.

Despite my views on equality in the kitchen, I couldn't quite escape the irritating "office girl" label. In the heavy equipment industry, the men called you a girl, no matter how old you were. Granted, I was only twenty-one, more girlish than the 40-somethings who worked in the main Accounting office two buildings away. But it still rankled me every time I heard Earl say "my office girl will take care of you" to our predominantly male clientele. Of course the men who brought their trucks in for repair always seemed to enjoy talking it up with me when settling their accounts, but I was smart enough to recognize their jovial camaraderie had more to do with the fact I was a slim woman with legs nice enough to wear short skirts, rather than a magna cum laude college student working to make ends meet.

Anyway, Jay Green, the new shop foreman Earl introduced that October Monday, was unquestionably handsome. And the cocky ass knew it. He had wavy chocolate brown hair and light sky blue eyes that reminded me of dawn in the Sierra Nevada. His thick mustache was blondish brown and curved slightly around his lips which somehow seemed to draw my wandering attention. Dressed like all the men in worn blue jeans, a button down chambray shirt, and steel-toed boots, Jay's tan face showed he was a guy who worked outdoors a lot. The weathered clothing almost, but not quite, hid a wide-shouldered physique, a muscular build his six-foot frame carried with confident ease.

"Nice to meet you, ma'am," Jay said, shaking my small hand with the end of his calloused fingers. I could tell by the way he looked through me he'd undoubtedly already forgotten my name.

"Nice to meet you too, Mr. Green," I smiled, performing the polite ritual as expected. Duty done, I waited for the men to wander back into the shop before calling my friend Rita Garcia who worked in the Parts Department across the parking lot.

"He's an ass," I announced.

"He's definitely got a damn fine ass," Rita observed, her New York accent punctuated by a heavy sigh, "I saw him getting out of his truck this morning when I drove in, so I stopped by and introduced my feisty self."

"Leave it to you, Ms. Garcia," I smothered a laugh. My friend appreciated men in all shapes and colors and never hesitated to let them know it.

"When I handed him my phone number, he acted all 'aw shucks ma'am', but I cut to the chase and told him his wedding ring wouldn't bother me none."

"Reets! You didn't!" Rita did not know the meaning of shy and she'd undoubtedly left demure in her rear view mirror in junior high.

"Worth a try," she said. "Ooops, gotta go Jess. Dave Higgins just walked in, and I swear the Viking looks better than he did last week."

Yes, I had to work with Jay Green, but I didn't have to like him. For the first month, he and I were all smiling politeness. Jay, treating me like I had the intelligence of a nine year-old by giving excruciatingly long and detailed explanations for tasks I knew like the back of my hand, ending the transaction with his patent smiling "Thank you, ma'am." Me, biting my tongue while he treated me as if I were painstakingly stupid in front of customers and coworkers, making no effort to hide my irritated "Really?" expression after he turned away. In my book, men who treated women like children and talked all sweet to their face typically said rude shit about them behind their backs.

Not that I cared what Jay said about me. Really, I didn't. But, well, I take that back. Actually I did care about whether he thought I was a brainless ditz, because clearly I wasn't, no matter how he might try to make me look like one. I'd grown up an only child with a dad who insisted on calling me his little Dum-Dum, which he swore was a term of endearment based on the lollipops I loved as a child, but became a name I considered a demeaning insult by the time I was twelve and had hated enough to prove him quite wrong. Jay Green, on the other hand, had probably barely finished high school, and if he did, he'd managed it on the coattails of some soft-hearted brainy girl who'd swooned when he looked her way. I wasn't a swooner and Jay's dum-dum treatment was getting under my skin big time.

One Wednesday in early November, Jay brought me a service order for Nowalk Transport, a strictly cash job for a company 90 days behind on their account. A sour Edgar Nowalk leaned on my service counter tapping his foot with his checkbook open as Jay detailed the billing instructions — as usual, stuff we'd gone over umpteen times. It didn't matter that I'd told the man just the week before I'd been preparing invoices efficiently since my second day on the job over a year ago, but he insisted on repeating the steps, looking at me with those smiling sky blue eyes. After Jay returned to the shop, I nodded to Nowalk and began quickly preparing the invoice until I noticed the hours didn't look quite right. I pulled the timesheet for the job and saw the error; Jay had charged Nowalk for two hours instead of the ten charged against the job.

"My apologies for the delay, Mr. Nowalk. I need to verify something here." I smiled my prettiest office girl smile. "I'll be just a moment." Leaving the grizzled man steaming at the counter, I pushed through the swinging double doors into the shop and strolled down the center aisle between the truck bays. Catcalls and whistles tracked my clicking high heels to the welding station, where I found Jay discussing an oddly shaped piece of metal with Jim Cairnes, my ex-boyfriend Kevin's wing man. Jimmy nodded at my approach, smothering a knowing grin when he saw my determined expression, but Jay frowned — obviously unhappy to see my slender self.

"This isn't right," I said, loud enough to be heard over the chattering power tools and rumbling truck motors. I waved a handful of dirt-stained papers.

"Whadda ya mean, it isn't right?' Jay stomped over to look at the documents in my hand. His face held an I-can't-believe-this-chick expression, one that made him look even more like an ass than usual.

"Jim here had two hours on the job fixing the undercarriage, but Kenny and Terry also booked time to repair the damage to the transmission ," I pointed at the timesheet. "It's ten hours, not two, which is kind of a big difference..."

"Lemme see that." Jay plucked the timesheet out of my hand and quickly scanned the figures.

I braced myself for an argument. I knew my records were accurate and was determined to prove it, but then he said the most remarkable thing: "You're right, Jess. I got interrupted as I was finalizing the bill. I saw Jim's two hours and marched on without double-checking. Sorry about that. I'll talk to Nowalk."

Touching me gently on the elbow, his calloused hand nudged me toward the office. A tingling sensation traveled up my arm, through, my shoulder, and straight down to my toes. I stumbled as I turned to stare at him, my eyes wide. He quickly steadied me by the arm. Funny thing was, I let him.

"I don't know how women walk in those things," he said, his lips smiling beneath the mustache.

"Me either," I mumbled, catching my balance and striding purposefully away. Stunned nearly speechless, my mind was busy trying to process the fact that Jay Green, the unequivocal pompous ass, had just admitted he was wrong and apologized. Nicely. To me. The office girl.

When we reached the office, I even let him open the swinging door for me — the whole southern gentleman thing. I was too distracted to protest, my body tingling with the memory of his touch, my mind recalling how the man had remembered my name and used it in a sentence. For goodness sakes. Would wonders never cease?

As it turned out, they sort of didn't.

Chapter Two

Thursday morning I arrived at the office at 8:05 am — right on time for me, five minutes late for Earl Wyse, who made a pretense of striding through the shop office right about that time and looking at his watch. Ignoring Earl, I yanked my rolling chair out from beneath my desk. To my surprise, the seat held a slim blue envelope. Ripping open the seal, I found an invitation to lunch with none other than Jay Green. His scrawling script was a mess as usual, but I'd cracked his handwriting code weeks back, so I had no problem reading it. The note said lunch was a 'thank you' for helping him with the Nowalk bill.

"He asked me to lunch," I whispered to Rita on the phone thirty seconds later.

"Afternoon delight, Jess? Way to go." Rita's low steamy chuckle reminded me of Mae West inviting gentlemen callers to her apartment for a little something more than conversation.

"Stop!" I blushed uncontrollably, my stomach fluttering at the memory of his touch. An image of strong tanned arms and long bare legs sprang to mind. "I'm not interested in *him*. He's an ass, remember? A married ass who thinks I'm dumber than a doornail."

"Maybe. Maybe not."

"Could you be any more obscure? I've only had one cup of coffee."

Rita sighed in mock frustration. "Jess, for God sakes! Yes, he may be just a regular everyday ass. But, then again, he may be a man acting like an ass because he doesn't know any other way to act. And although he IS technically a married ass, sometimes things are not as they appear."

"What the hell is that supposed to mean?" I took a sip of coffee and shook my head. Rita's pragmatic philosophy on men was often convoluted, but some days she was downright insightful, and if today was one of those days, I wanted to hear more. I needed all the help I could get.

"OK. Number one: Jess even you have to admit he's a downright fox."

"Well... yes. OK. He's just about the best looking man this side of the Mississippi, but—"

"Number two," Rita interrupted. "Do you even get how much it took for him to admit his mistake to you? In front of other people no less? A lot of men would have blown you off without a second thought, but he didn't. And he apologized. Think about that."

"But, Reets..."

Speaking over my weak protest, Rita continued. "Number three: a lunch invitation is way above and beyond the call of duty. Men don't go through all that trouble unless there's somethin' else going on. For now, he can hide his interest behind a thanks-for-the-help excuse. And if lunch turns out to be simply lunch, that's where it'll end. But guys like Jay Green don't waste time on lunch unless there's something in it for them. That somethin' is you, silly." Rita took a deep breath and waited patiently for my brain to process her wisdom.

"You think he's interested in *me*? Like *that kind of interested*?" I ran my fingers through my long dark hair, wondering how I'd missed the cue.

"Duh. Earth to Jess??? Come in, Jess. Why else would he go so far out of his way to spend so much time with you?" Rita's throaty laugh wafted over the phone line.

"Well... but..." Something inside me felt like the world was tipping sideways. I'd spent over a month convincing myself Jay was a Texas hick who thought I had the brains of a third grader and probably couldn't stand the sight of me — not to mention his manner toward women had stalled in a 1950's time warp. In two short minutes, Rita had summarily painted his behavior in an entirely different light, a scenario where Jay was showing

18

his romantic interest in me the only way he knew how.

Oh my God... I'd been so certain he was simply a chauvinistic red-neck, I never even considered another option. What if Jay actually did like me? What if all his smiling conversation over billing had been an excuse to hang out with me?

"Shitfire, Reets. What if you're right?" I nervously twirled my chair around in a circle, one black high heel dragging lightly across the linoleum floor.

"IF? Think about it. You really think there's an IF here?" Rita hooted the question as if the answer was a foregone conclusion.

"OK... maybe not. But it couldn't possibly ever go anywhere. I'd never sleep with a married man." The 'no married men' rule had always been chiseled in concrete for me. I couldn't ever see myself meddling in another woman's marriage.

"Never say never, honey." Rita's clipped New York accent turned the nevers into 'nevahs.' "Life is too damned short for never."

Although I was a believer in Rita's 'never say never' sentiment, I wasn't ready to consider the possibility my long-held rule around married men could ever topple. I'd been raised to think people who had affairs outside their marriage were simply low- down cheats and if they could lie to their spouse, they'd lie about anything. Firmly ensconced my ivory tower, I thought there was no excuse for it. My mother's Catholic background had enforced this attitude, making me think of marriage as if it were some type of prison without hope of parole, not to mention the fact infidelity was considered a sin — adultery was what they called it which always struck me as kind of an odd term. Explained a lot about why I wasn't married and didn't really plan to be until at least forty. Except if I decided to have kids, because that commitment definitely required two parents. And except when I lost all good sense and for one glorious Sonoma summer convinced myself Kevin McMahon was someone special enough to consider marrying, but that was before I woke up, smelled reality, and broke up with the self-absorbed jerk.

See, I'd always believed love was a veritable force of nature, and you couldn't really put a fence around it or say it's OK to love these folks, but not these. Yet religion painted these lines around who you could and couldn't love. So did families and our prominent Western culture, weird socioeconomic and color lines which I admit I'd outright ignored for most of my life. But the adultery rule had been important to my mother, probably because all the men in her family had been womanizers and all the women in her family had patiently endured their baloney and years of hurt. So, I'd always stayed well away from married men so as not to test my resolve. Better to never have to admit I was someone's "other woman" to my mom; I don't think she'd ever forgive me for that indiscretion.

Yet sometimes, in the light of new information, even the most well-ingrained personal rules can be broken.

Easy to say now. As if I could have made a different choice. But the thing is, I didn't. Jay and I didn't. I don't think we could have.

Chapter Three

The lunch date began at noon sharp. Jay pulled up in front of my office door in his old blue Ford 150 pickup and opened the passenger door. Shouldering my purse, I gave my outfit one last inspection to ensure nothing was amiss. The sleeveless red sheath Rita insisted I borrow for the occasion was almost, but not quite, too short for my taste. ("Fits like a glove," she'd pronounced this morning in the rest room as she'd tugged the scoop neck lower to expose my cleavage. "He'll be squirming in his seat.) Frankly, I didn't know if I wanted Jay squirming in his seat. But I figured looking one's best never hurt, and the shapely red dress guaranteed I'd earn well above a 'C' grade.

The Willie Nelson Band serenaded our drive to Vicente's Bistro, Jay unselfconsciously humming *My Heroes Have Always Been Cowboys* under his breath. Although he hadn't said much to me all day, every time I glanced over at him his eyes were looking at my dress instead of the road.

Once at the restaurant, Jay seemed to shed his uncharacteristically quiet demeanor and began to make conversation.

"I wanted to thank you, Jess. For catching that mistake with the Nowalk billing, of course. But also, you know for all you do there at the shop. You're pretty good at it."

"You sound surprised that I'd be good at it," I smiled, half teasing, and he took it in stride, smiling back, sky blue eyes alight.

"Nah. It's just I've seen some pretty incompetent office staff in my time around the block. You're different. Way different. So, tell me about yourself. What are you taking in night school? Sonoma State, right?"

Jay studied me with interest. I sensed his sincerity, accompanied by a focused intensity I hadn't noticed before. He treated me as if I were the most important thing in the room, really listening to what I said, his attention devoted to me and only me — not the giggling office workers the next table over smiling in his direction, or the pretty painted housewives surreptitiously admiring his physique. As our eyes met across the table, I reconsidered everything I'd ever thought about this man, every cliché judgment I'd fostered, every half-assed assumption I'd made. Jay Green was simply himself, without frills or pretense, and

I found being with him, talking with him, laughing with him surprisingly easy.

Our conversation followed the standard getting-to-know-you path: where I lived, what I was studying (how'd he find out I was in school?), how the hell I ended up at the in the Sonoma Diesel shop office. At first I kept my answers short: living in Santa Rosa, Social Work major, job placement courtesy of AccTemps Employment Agency. But then I filled in a few other details to answer the questions he hadn't asked — my own apartment, no roommate, no steady boyfriend as of mid-September, when a nasty fight over my willingness to use my hard-earned money to buy gas for his boat, ended my year-long relationship with Kevin Mac (who had always liked the fact I made a decent wage, perhaps more than he actually liked me come to think of it, and no woman in their right mind wants to put up with that bull-hickey, right?).

After we ordered the manicotti lunch special, I turned the tables and asked Jay some of the same questions. As he relaxed in my company, conversation spun easily between us and he became more animated. Beyond the fact I'm a good listener, I found myself fascinated by this handsome man's life story. The world beyond our lunch table simply disappeared. I couldn't have told you how full the restaurant was, or our waiter's name, but I'll always remember where we sat and how the light from the stained glass patio doors fell across our table, painting a rainbow across the white linen.

"Grew up in a little town named Canyon, just outside Amarillo, Texas where I played cornerback for the Canyon Eagles. Didn't have much when I was a kid 'cept ice cream on Saturday night and church on Sunday." Jay smiled at the memory, his southern accent turning the word Amarillo into Amarilluh. "Broke my arm down in San Antonio riding rodeo when I was nineteen. Candy and I'd been married about a year and needed the extra cash 'cause our baby daughter Ellie was sick a lot. I was just an apprentice mechanic then, and my salary didn't cover the mortgage *and* all the doctor bills. We lost our home and nearly our car because I couldn't work for a few months. After the arm healed, I didn't have a lot of choices if I wanted to provide for my family, so I joined the Army, which at least got my daughter the medical care she needed. But after two deployments, El grew up really not knowing me." Jay paused to look out the window, his brow furrowed.

"That must have been hard," I said. "When you came back, though, she got a chance to know you."

"She did," Jay nodded, pursing his lips. "But first I had to explain I was her real daddy, not the man Candy'd been seeing while I was gone."

"Oh," I said, my fork hand freezing in mid-air. "I'm sorry."

"Me too," Jay agreed, pushing ricotta-filled shells around on his plate. "But we got through it,

Candy and I. Talked about divorce, but decided against it. Thing is, we got married too young. She was 17 and pregnant. I was barely 18. Our parents were religious, and pretty much insisted on the wedding and we went along with it. I thought it was only the right thing to do, you know. But it wasn't. Not really. Not for either one of us. 'Cept we didn't know how to say 'stop' at the time. Or make a different choice."

Jay took a bite and shrugged. "Sounds like one of those sad country songs, don't it."

"Real life, real people." I raised my eyebrows and gazed up into his face. "We play the cards we're dealt, yeah?"

"You got that right," Jay sniffed, then looked into my eyes and smiled a sad smile. "But sometimes there's no getting past the things that happen, the choices we make. Candy and I tried every way we knew how. Our second daughter, Gracie, is five years younger than Ellie. We had a few good years there in Texas. I was making OK money, the girls were growing like bean plants." Jay shook his head. He fell silent then, as if he was considering what to say next.

"What happened then?"

"My buddy Dave Higgins is what happened then. We moved up to Redding the year Ellie started fourth grade. Job opportunity I couldn't pass up."

"Dave Higgins?" Curious to learn whether the Dave Jay was talking about was the same guy Rita had a crush on, I cocked my head in interest.

"Met Dave in boot camp. We served in the same unit overseas. Stayed in contact after our tours were up. When a job at Caterpillar came open in Redding, he gave me a call and said 'get your ass up here.' He'd arranged a sit-down with his uncle, the Service Manager. Sounded worth it. I drove nearly two days straight to get there." Laughing, Jay turned his coffee cup around in the saucer.

"As it turned out, the effort was worth it. Pay raise, signing bonus, moving allowance. I got Candy and the girls moved into a rental house within the month. I *thought* we were starting a new life, away from everything that happened in Texas. Like we were getting a second chance."

"You *were* starting a new life, right?"

"Yes and no." Jay rubbed his forehead. "*I* was starting a new life. *Candy* was going back to an old life. Before I knew it, she and Dave are all over each other every chance they could get. I couldn't fucking believe it.... But then again, this is Candy we're talkin' 'bout and she was maybe making up for all those teenage years taking care of a sick baby. I dunno. Anyway, Dave's wife Gina and I figured 'why not' so we hooked up too. I guess that's what they call swingers or something, trading partners..."

Jay gazed at me as if to test my response to the term.

27

"I guess," I said, not sure what he expected me to say. "If that's what you're into..."

"Yeah, well the thing is, I wasn't. Not really. Those Redding years were just a lot of wasted days and wasted nights partying. Don't get me wrong, Gina was a great gal. Devastated when Dave started running around like a high school kid with Candy on his arm. She jumped into bed with me for somethin' to do, or to make her husband jealous, or whatever. I don't blame her. I blame myself for getting mixed up in the whole thing. I was lonely and thought maybe.... well, it don't matter anymore." Jay paused.

I could tell he wasn't quite done with what he had to say, so I prompted him. "Fast forward a few years and you're here in Sonoma now. Candy here too?"

"Yup... Her affair with Dave ended earlier this year. We moved down last month when I was offered the foreman position. But things aren't really right between us. Kinda hard to pick up where we left off again, although we're trying."

"And Dave? He's moved here now too, right? Works for Nowalk?"

"Yeah, he ended up over in Glen Allen. A bachelor now. Gina divorced him. Had enough of his bull. Thing is, Dave and I were friends through a pretty intense couple of years. Looked out for each other when things got dicey. Can't erase that."

Jay took a deep breath and looked at me. His eyes held an intense determination I hadn't seen before, a rawness that stripped away the polite Southern facade to reveal a man who felt things quite deeply, however casual he made it all sound. Then he blushed and shook his head, eyes downcast, his expression suddenly turning to that of a man desperately scrabbling backward as if to undo what was already done.

"Jay," I said, resting my hand atop his on the white table cloth. "Don't—"

"I'm sorry, Jess," he interrupted. "I can't believe I told you this pitiful story...."

My thin fingers clenched his muscled wrist as if to pull him back from whatever abyss he was staring into. Without rational explanation, I could feel his despair and pain as if it were my own. "Don't second-guess yourself. Or your choices." Before I knew it, my other hand was unconsciously reaching across the table as if to touch his face. I stopped before I actually made contact with his skin, but not before Jay's fingers caught mine. The sun traced golden strands amongst his wavy brown curls, matching the blond-brown mustache. His hand felt warm and safe, the intimacy eerily familiar.

Studying our entwined fingers, Jay frowned. "You know, I never told anyone that entire story before. I guess it's been stuck inside me, twisting in my gut. Maybe it was time to tell it. Or maybe... it's just you." His eyes looked into mine with a disarming intensity and, God help me, I tumbled hopelessly into the sky blue depths. My lungs swelled with that same weightless sensation you feel when you crest the top of the roller coaster track and begin the plunge down the other side.

What was I getting myself into?

Two hours later, Rita showed up at my counter and insisted I accompany her outside for a cigarette break. We stood shivering in the weak autumn sun on the empty Parts Department loading dock, "What the hell happened?" she asked for the third time, lighting a second Kool cigarette off her first. Her svelte frame was draped in fabulous form-fitting fuchsia, a cropped black cashmere sweater curving around her shapely shoulders.

As my friend blew intersecting smoke rings, I paced beside the concrete wall, trying to find the words to describe lunch with Jay. "It was nice," I said, shrugging. "Vicente's manicotti was great as usual. We talked... that's it."

"That ain't all of it. I'm calling bullshit," Rita pronounced, her sharp eyes scrutinizing my best nonchalant office girl expression.

"Reets, I swear, we just talked. You know, the polite who-are-you type of conversation people who don't know each other have at lunch. It was... interesting." I stopped there, certain that if I said anything more Rita would instantly pry open the lid on the jar of confused emotion I was madly trying to contain.

"You talked? That's it? For two and a half hours. Yeah, right." Rita rolled her dark eyes. "Like I was born yesterday."

"What do you want to hear? That we were doing it like rabbits in the front seat of his truck down by the Cashew Creek?" I tipped my head and frowned at her in exasperation. "Don't get all a-twitter. We didn't."

Rita gave me her older-friend-knows-best look. "OK... so what am I picking up on here? *Something* happened. I know you, Jessica Carline Maneiro, and I know when you are trying to *pretend* nothing is happening and getting all twing-dangled up in your head. So, for chrissakes just tell me already..."

"Twing-dangled? Is that a word?" I emitted a weak chuckle at my friend's creative vocabulary.

"Don't change the subject." Rita stomped one Italian high heel on the pavement.

"Gawd, Reets. I can't tell you if I don't even know myself."

Rita looked at me questioningly, one painted eyebrow raised, a clear invitation for me to say more.

"You're right. *Something* happened. I don't know what it was. There was this weird space/time thing where I sort of lost track of what was happening around me and got so focused on him and our conversation.... It was if we'd known each other for like, years... and, I dunno, Reets, then he grabbed my hand in his and said "*I've never told anyone that before. Maybe it was time. Or maybe it's just you."* which in that moment made me feel like there was this intense connection between us... And then he paid the bill and we left." I paused, totally out of words to describe what couldn't possibly be described. Shaking my head, I shrugged again. "Fuck. I don't know what happened. It doesn't make sense. I barely know the man." I turned and paced to the end of the loading dock where the November breeze whipped my long hair into tangles.

Rita's hand on my elbow made me startle. I turned to see my friend standing beside me, clutching her black cashmere sweater around her shoulders for warmth. Her dark eyes held a concerned expression. "Sorry Jess. Didn't mean to push. You know—"

"It's OK," I said, earnestly, signaling an end to the conversation. "I gotta get back to work."

Rita ignored my interruption and kept right on talking. "— all those things you described. Losing track of the world. Feeling like you know him well, even when all the evidence says you don't. That intense connection that makes no logical sense. Some people say those same things when they talk about the experience of falling in love."

Gazing into my friend's face, I felt a hollow sickly feeling in my gut. "That can't happen," I said. "No way. No how." Without so much as a good-bye, I turned and walked across the parking lot toward my office as fast as my high heels would permit.

From across the parking lot, Rita's low voice reached my ears. Her tone was kind in only the way a friend's voice can sound when telling you a hard truth you'd rather not hear. "It's already happened, hon. No gettin' that back into the box."

Chapter Four

For a week I avoided being alone with Jay. I stayed professional and polite in the office. Said 'good morning' and all that. But I didn't make eye contact. I guess I didn't trust myself to look into his sapphire blues again without feeling that undeniable connection I didn't want to feel. I couldn't allow myself to feel anything like that because our relationship could never go anywhere. I wished I could pretend lunch never happened and he was still just an asshole foreman who irritated the crap out of me. Friday afternoon I stayed late to catch up the payroll hours and make things easy on the front office to cut checks the following Wednesday, the day before Thanksgiving. The company didn't have to do it, but they usually did, sort of a surprise to hand out the pay checks two days early with a frozen turkey, a holiday gift for the men's families.

At 6 pm, Earl Wyse strolled through the lobby with his battered tin lunch box under his arm. "You and Jay are the only ones left. I'll lock the front on my way out, so when you leave just make sure the door closes tight behind you."

"Will do. Thanks." I nodded and went back to my keyboard. "I'll be done here in a few."

Earl jangled his keys, then stopped at the counter. "And thanks for staying late on a Friday. I know the accounting girls will appreciate the effort." Embarrassed at handing out a compliment, the bearded man quickly left and I returned to work, determined to get through the timecards so I could get the hell out of there.

When I heard the swinging doors to the shop creak open, I was donning my raincoat. Had to be Jay, damn it. If I'd just been five minutes quicker, I could have avoided seeing him and been on my way. But now I had to say *something* to the man. I couldn't just run away from him.

"You still here, Jess?"

"Yup. Just got done. Grabbing my purse and heading out now."

Jay padded around the corner and stopped at the service counter. "I'd like to apologize again for our lunch conversation."

"Jay, I—"

"Let me finish, please. I made you uncomfortable and that's not what I intended. I thought..." He looked at me directly then, eyes serious. "Well, I ah... I thought we might be able to be friends. That is, if you want to be."

Relieved, I smiled a genuine smile, my eyes now unafraid to meet his. "Of course. I'd like that. Very much." Friends. That I could do. Absolutely. After all, there was nothing wrong with being friends with a male coworker. That lunch experience — the feelings that swamped me when he touched my hand — that would never happen again. I wouldn't let it. Or so I told myself.

"Good," he said, smiling back, the gold-brown mustache quirking up at the sides. "Since it's already so late, ya wanna join me for a bite to eat. Maybe a pizza? As a friend, of course."

"OK," I said, surprised, but not altogether displeased. "If you let me buy. And it has to be Olivetti's. They make the best pizza in town." Remarkably, my voice sounded normal. Inside I was relieved to find that I wasn't feeling all twing-dangled any longer. Of course Jay and I could be friends.

"Olivetti's it is." Jay nodded. "Meet you there in 15 minutes."

The pizza parlor was filled to the rafters with noisy patrons. Jay managed to nab a table from a departing family and we settled into opposite seats in the fake red leather booth with a laugh.

"Better to be lucky than good," he grinned, helping me push aside the previous occupants' plates.

Our fingers brushed accidentally. making me startle as if I'd been burned. I glanced up at his face for a moment, wondering if he'd felt it too. Jay busied himself mopping up pizza crumbs with a napkin, avoiding eye contact. We sat for a moment in awkward silence while I wracked my brain trying to think up a safe topic of conversation. Something friends would talk about.

"Beer?" he finally said, taking out his wallet.

"I'm buying," I insisted.

"You're buying the pizza. I'm buying the beer." Jay stood and casually picked his way through the crowd toward the bar. I silently admired his backside as he walked away. *Friends can admire friends' backsides*, I thought, smiling to myself.

I studied the menu for something to do, fidgeting in the oversize booth. I always ordered the same thing — Olivetti's Meatsa Masterpiece — so checking other menu options was purely me trying to manage nerve sputters. A line began forming in the restaurant foyer, people willing to wait for an open table. Jay and I had arrived just in time to avoid the same grisly fate.

Suddenly above the crowd's rumble, I heard a woman's New York accent. "Jessica Carline!"

I raised my eyes from the menu to see a beatific Rita dodging tables, a bemused Dave Higgins in tow.

Sliding into the opposite seat, Rita winked at me and yanked the grinning Dave down beside her. "Mind if we join you? Dave, you know Jess, right?"

"Sure do," Dave smiled, his chiseled Nordic features on full display.

"Wow. Yeah. Well, HI!" I stumbled my way through the words, wondering how the hell to tell my best friend she couldn't sit with me. Especially when the table was big enough for four and you weren't out on a date with a new beau or anything that would preclude being friendly and polite.

"You here with Kevie Mac? I saw his Chevy out in the parking lot." Rita cocked her head, then snuggled up against Dave's side in a manner beyond friendly.

"No. Actually I'm here with a friend." I said, trying to decide the best way to deliver the fact my friend was Jay Green while my eyes scanned the crowd looking for Kevin, who I hadn't seen in over two months — probably because I rarely, if ever, went anywhere I knew he frequented. Olivetti's on a Friday night was 50/50, so it would not surprise me if Kev were here somewhere in the crowd. Nerves sputtered through me all over again as my friend eyed me suspiciously, one painted eyebrow raised.

"Hi, Rita," Jay said, plunking two beers on the table and sitting his fine backside on the seat beside me. "How's it, Dave?"

Rita's dark eyes boggled in outraged surprise. For once the woman was speechless. I clenched my teeth to keep from laughing aloud at her comedic expression, an expression that clearly said "What the hell!?" to anyone who knew her even remotely well.

Dave, on the other hand, took the news in stride. "Good to see ya, Jay," he said, extending his huge hand.

"For sure." Jay grasped his old friend's outstretched palm and shook it warmly as if it was just another day in the neighborhood. "So what's good here, Jess? I was looking at that Meatsa. What do you think?"

Dinner was a hootenanny — really any event that included Rita Garcia on the guest list was a hootenanny — but brawny Dave Higgins proved her consummate match. The two were so hilarious, I wondered fleetingly if they shouldn't do comedy together. Jay and I were in stitches the entire evening listening to their banter. Amazingly, we only spilled one beer at our table, that entirely due to Dave's arm gesturing wildly to describe an injured goose who refused to be retrieved and attacked his hunting dog the previous Sunday. Scared the bejeezus out of the poor thing, and sent it scurrying under the truck with his tail tucked.

"Call the dog shrink!" Rita declared. "You're gonna need professional help if you ever want that dog to retrieve anything ever again."

"I think it's too soon to tell whether there's any permanent mental damage," Dave said with a perfectly straight face. "But I'll keep your recommendation in mind, Ms. Meter."

"Ms. Meter?" I looked at Rita with a raised eyebrow.

"Lovely Rita Meter Maid," Dave smiled at the woman beside him, then waggled his bushy blonde eyebrows. "May I inquire discretely. When are you free to have some fun with me?"

Rita unabashedly batted her eyelashes and we all laughed at Dave's twist on the Beatles lyrics.

"We're headed down to the Riverrun Tavern tonight. You guys should come. Jim Mason Band is playing." Rita posed the invitation as she intertwined her manicured fingers with Dave's rough ones.

"Thanks, but I don't think—" I began.

"Jim Mason? From up Redding way?" Jay interrupted.

"Yup. The very same," Dave confirmed, nodding down at Rita with a devilish grin.

"Haven't seen those guys in a while," Jay said. "We could go for a little bit. Jess?"

"OK. Sure." I shrugged in agreement. Couldn't hurt to watch a band play a set at the Riverrun. After that, I'd excuse myself and go home. No big deal.

Chapter Five

The following morning I awoke to the sound of a squirrel chattering on my bedroom balcony. The nutty rodent was carrying on a one-sided conversation, berating someone or something I could not see from my prone position. Every so often he'd stop and utter a series of "Tchaaa, tchaaa, tchaaa" sounds and flick his long tail back and forth, then he'd scamper up the wrought iron railing and back down again. Since I did not speak squirrel, I had no idea what the deal was, but the sound was unquestionably irritating.

Reaching across the bed, I grabbed my extra pillow and tossed it at the sliding glass door. "Quiet!"

Instead of running off or at least simmering down, the damn thing turned his ire on me, his beady eyes staring at me through the window. "Tchaaa, tchaaa, tchaaa," it scolded, fluffy gray tail twitching.

"What the fuck is your problem?" I sputtered to the rodent as I stumbled out of bed toward the kitchen. Making an about-face at the door frame, I returned to the bedroom to retrieve my bathrobe so as not to flash my inquisitive neighbors.

After the previous night's festivities, I had enough problems of my own beyond one scolding squirrel. Perched on a rickety wooden stool at my breakfast bar, I sipped a cup of watery instant coffee and gazed through my bedroom door at my empty messy bed, remembering all too clearly how it had not been so empty a few hours earlier. Not so empty at all. In fact, it had been delightfully occupied by a handsome man I'd sworn I'd never sleep with in a thousand years. But no way, no how, was I regretting my choice or the fact I'd broken my own "no married men" rule. Thankfully I was sitting down so I could catch my breath while the memories of the night before flooded my mind and the resulting weakness in my knees could pass without dumping me onto the carpeted floor.

Speaking of the floor, I turned to face the living room and blushed. The mess there consisted mostly of blankets and sofa cushions and two telltale Heineken beer bottles abandoned half full.

What the hell had I been thinking?

The answer was all too obvious: I hadn't been thinking — at least not all that clearly. No, that wasn't entirely accurate. I couldn't in good conscience make any excuses for my behavior. I *had* been thinking, all right, and I'd decided to let consequences be damned. Last night I hadn't cared about tomorrow or the next day; all I cared about was Jay. Jay and I. Us. All I cared about was us, and the wonderful soaring feeling that being with him gave me.

Perhaps it had been inevitable. Or perhaps I was simply one of those "other women" who had affairs with married low-down cheating men. Didn't matter.

Rita's invitation to go to Riverrun Tavern was the beginning of the end to Jay's and my friendship. Not that we were no longer friends, but we were well downstream from that label. Anyway, he and I were listening to the Jim Mason band while Rita and Dave made out on the other side of the table, when the lead guitarist struck the beginning licks to Jay's favorite Willie Nelson tune.

"Come on," Jay'd said, grabbing me by the hand and up out of my seat.

My first inclination had been to politely refuse, but then common sense prevailed and I figured it was just a dance. No harm in that, right?

I'd never been so wrong in my life.

Looking back the morning after, I figured if it hadn't been a slow dance — or even if it had been a slow dance, but a different song — the evening would have turned out different. But the thing was, Jay and I were there in that place at that moment in time together, and what happened, happened. The lyrics to *My Heroes Have Always Been Cowboys* hit close to home for Jay, close to his heart, and when he gathered me into his arms, his heart became my heart. There's no other way to describe it. That same thing that happened in the restaurant when he touched my hand happened again, where the world faded away and it was just him and me, as if we'd always been together. As if there had always been an us.

And nothing else mattered.

"*Sadly in search of, and one step in back of, themselves and their slow movin' dreams.*" Jay whispered the lyrics in my ear as the song ended. Then he pulled back and looked into my eyes, and what he said next changed whatever friendship we might have forged forever. "I been dreamin' 'bout someone like you Jess. Since way before I met you... I been alone so long, and now that we're here, I just..." He stopped speaking then, and kissed me. And kept kissing me, because I'd melted against him and was kissing him back.

We left Dave and Rita at that corner table in the club without saying good-bye and the rest of our adventurous evening resulted in the mess I was looking at in my apartment that very moment.

Now what? I thought in the shower, dreading Monday morning although it was still two days away. I'd broken my own "no married men" rule and I'd done it with someone I worked with. How dumb was that? How was I supposed to I face a man I've just boinked all night in a work setting and pretend we're nothing but colleagues?

Always eager to share her delectable weekend report, Rita showed up at my office door at 8:07 Monday morning, her Cheshire cat grin beaming. Dressed in an emerald green pantsuit over an ivory lace camisole, she handed me a fresh cup of black coffee, then leaned her elbows on the service counter. "How was *your* weekend?"

"Good," I said, smiling my practiced office girl smile hoping Rita didn't notice. "Yours?"

"Fucking awesome," she gushed, then launched into the tale of Dave Higgins asking her out and spending the weekend at his place in Glen Allen, and how funny he was, and what a great time they'd had. In more ways than one. In every way imaginable.

"Jess, are you listening?" Rita's question penetrated my foggy brain ten minutes later.

"Absolutely," I smiled from the safety of my office chair. "Sounds wonderful, Reets. He's functional *and* ornamental, a great combination if you ask me. The best type of boyfriend to have. Especially since he has a job."

"You got that right," Rita smiled, her dark eyes sparkling way brighter than I'd seen them in months. "I didn't know Jay and Dave were friends, but I guess they go way back, huh?"

"Yeah. I guess," I said, then began straightening some file folders in my inbox.

"You OK?" Rita turned her high-beam eyes on me. "Where exactly did you two go after you left us at the Riverrun Friday?"

45

"Home. I went home." I said the words as convincingly casual as I dared. It wasn't exactly that I didn't want Rita to know, it was more that I didn't really want to talk about my weekend in the office where anyone could walk in and overhear.

Speeding around the counter, Rita stood beside my desk, her dark eyes narrowing. "Stand up," she insisted.

Unable to resist her big sister voice, I promptly did, teetering slightly on my high heels.

"Why are you wearing loose jeans and that baggy, ratty sweater to work?"

"What's wrong with this sweater?" I said, feigning outrage. "My mother gave me this sweater for my birthday last year."

"Exactly. It's middle-age housewife comfort clothes and you know it. Where is your eye shadow and lipstick? Are you sick or something?"

"NO! For goodness sakes, Reets... I felt casual today, so I dressed down. No big deal."

"Alright already. Cheese whilikers, girl. Come on, let's go over to Accounting and steal some of their hazelnut creamer." Rita grabbed me by the elbow and propelled me around the counter through the Service Department lobby.

"I don't use creamer."

"No, but I do," she smiled. "Walk with me." Rita opened the glass door and held her manicured hand out in invitation.

Whatever, I thought and strolled past her. The errand would take five minutes. I walked into the parking lot and turned to Rita, only to find her a good eight steps behind me.

"I thought we were going to Accounting to steal creamer." I stopped and waited for her to catch up.

"We are," Rita said, grinning at me. "I just wanted to confirm something first."

"I'm lost here, Reets. What are you talking about? Confirm what exactly?" Rita's shenanigans were proving too challenging for me first thing on a Monday morning and I was losing patience.

"I wanted to confirm you spent at least one night this weekend fucking your brains out with Jay Green and are still sore in the legs from all the fun." Rita sauntered past me, chin high, as if she'd just won the Nobel Peace Prize in Body Language Analysis. "Tell me it ain't true. "

Groaning, I raked my hands through my still damp hair. "Is it that obvious?" I wailed, my voice cracking with the strain.

"Not on you," Rita assured me. "But if you'd seen Jay this morning, there'd be no doubt in your mind the man had been well and truly fucked quite recently. The shit-eating grin on his face gave it away. I knew the second I laid eyes on him he'd been to heaven for the first time in a long time. And I guessed heaven might look a little bit like you."

Rita gently put her hand on my arm. "But I didn't think you'd be this upset about it. What's wrong? Did he hurt you?" She studied me closely, her huge brown eyes meeting mine.

"No. Nothing like that," I immediately shook my head. "Not at all. It was amazing. Better than amazing. But I don't know how I'm supposed to see him at work without.... Everyone's gonna know, right?" I suddenly felt acutely embarrassed thinking about Early Wyse and the entire shop — including Kevin's friends Jim and Terry — staring at me knowing I'd been to bed with the new foreman.

"No one is going to know for sure unless someone tells them, but folks may guess," Rita nodded. "I'll tell you what though, everyone already knows Jay and Candy have one of those "open" marriage arrangements. That whole business with Dave and Gina." Rita flapped her hand in the air. "Dave told me all about it this weekend. Gossip from Redding to Sonoma travels faster than you might think."

"Shitfire," I said, taking a deep breath. "What have I gotten myself into?"

"Nothing to beat yourself up over, sweetie. You wanted to. He wanted to. You're both consenting adults. Don't forget, Candy doesn't want Jay. If she did, she wouldn't be fucking around on him every few years. With their history, I'm figuring he'll tell her, so it ain't gonna be a secret where someone's being betrayed and hurt — not if their marriage is as "open" as it seems she's always insisted it was. Folks who are all prim and religious and shit will say you'll be damned to hell for screwing the guy, but that's eighteenth century thinking. Come on."

Rita linked her arm with mine and pulled me along. We meandered across the tarmac together, quiet for a few moments. Dark rain clouds hovered over the coastal hills, promising a shower by lunchtime.

"You like him a lot, huh?"

Rita's question didn't entirely surprise me. My friend could be amazingly perceptive at times.

"Yeah, Reets. I do." And that was precisely the problem. I probably liked Jay Green way too much for my own good. But then we don't always get to pick who we love. Sometimes it just happens when we least expect it.

Chapter Six

The next few months Jay and I lived a version of Kenny Rogers *Daytime Friends and Nighttime Lovers:* working at the shop weekdays, pizza Friday nights, and talking and making love into the early hours Saturday mornings until he headed home to his family. I'd fallen for a man who understood me in a way no one else ever had, someone who thought I was smart and funny, someone who really listened to what I said and thought my interests and opinions were important. Jay was a man who I found I respected — for what he'd made out of his life despite his lean childhood , for his commitment to doing the right thing even when it was difficult, for his keen knowledge and expertise in his field. Working with him, I got to see Jay was a good boss, demanding, but fair, always encouraging, but not one to put up with shirking or inattentive mistakes. Somewhere along the line, he'd become a good leader, a man other men respected and willingly followed.

Some people undoubtedly thought our arrangement was twisted, that I was some kind of seductress stealing Jay away from his home life, or that Jay was some kind of playboy getting a piece of ass on the side. Others just thought Jay and Candy were doing one of those "open marriage" things again and I was a naive little college girl he'd talked into their swingers game — him being ten years older and wiser and me being so young, dumb, and gullible. Those were just a few of the comments we heard through the grapevine. In the absence of information, folks will make up a story just to have something interesting to gossip about. People painted us with a dirty brush because they could. But our relationship wasn't even remotely like what anyone imagined.

Not at all.

Jay and I were simply enjoying every minute we had. Not talking about the future. Just staying in the now. Because now was all we had.

One late Friday night in January before he headed home, Jay pulled a paperback novel out of his Carhart coat pocket and handed it to me. *The Reincarnation of Peter Proud* by Max Ehrlich.

"What's this?" I said, thumbing the worn pages. Although I believed in reincarnation, I didn't usually read those paranormal suspense novels that skewed metaphysical concepts into horror stories.

"I found this on Candy's bookshelf a month or so back. I actually read it. I don't read very fast, so it took me a long time. But I want you to read it. Please." Jay's blue eyes were serious.

"OK. You want me to read it because..." I knew there was more to his out-of-left-field request.

"Because I think it explains a lot," Jay said, collecting his truck keys from the breakfast bar. "About us."

He gathered me into his arms and kissed me on the forehead. "Will you?"

"Sure," I said, snuggling against his muscular frame. "And then I want to hear what you really think about it. Deal?"

"Deal. Love you, babe."

"Love you too," I said, reluctantly releasing him. A moment later his boot steps echoed in the stairwell as he descended into the rainy night.

The next day I spent the morning in the Sonoma State library conducting research for my Social Psychology paper. The rain had left the campus drenched and dripping, creating ponds out of potholes and permeating the air with a soggy chill. The library grew busier as morning waned into afternoon, so I gathered some books into my oversize backpack and headed home, determined to get the assignment off the ground, if not a handful of pages drafted.

The baseboard heater in my apartment protested against working overtime, so I turned on the oven for few minutes for a quick blast of heat. Wrapping myself into an oversize sweater, I brewed a cup of licorice tea and studied the psychology tomes now stacked in three neat piles on my breakfast bar. *Better get to it,* I thought, my hand grabbing the book atop the shortest stack on my way to my sagging oversized living room sofa.

The couch was positioned with a view out the wide front windows, its back kitty-corner to the entryway. I settled into the voluminous cushions beneath my rainbow granny-square afghan and took a luscious sip of tea, letting the smooth licorice warmth fill my chest. Rain beat against the windows, drops driven sideways by the gusty wind — a good day to be indoors. Expecting Caccioppo's *Attitudes and Persuasions*, I opened the book in my lap only to find Ehrlich's *The Reincarnation of Peter Proud.*

Fine, I thought, accepting the inadvertent diversion, *I'll read the first chapter.* At least then I could say I started the book if Jay asked. Three hours later I reached the end of Part I: Proud had found the town he'd seen in his dream in Massachusetts, the place he'd lived before he died, but he didn't yet know his name from that lifetime.

I had to hand it to Ehrlich, the way he braided together murder mystery, life after death, and romantic tragedy had totally captured my attention. Collecting my cold teacup where I'd abandoned it on the coffee table, I meandered into the kitchen and set it in the microwave for a warm-up, then scanned the epigraphs that began Part II:

Except that a man be born again, he cannot see the Kingdom of God. — Christ

God generates beings, and then sends them back over and over again, till they return to him. — The Koran

After all, it is no more surprising to be born twice than it is to be born once. Everything in Nature is resurrection. — Voltaire

Death is but a sleep and a forgetting. If death is not prelude to another life, the intermediate period is a cruel mockery. — Gandhi

I was already familiar with most of these quotes, the exception being the one from The Koran. I hadn't studied the Islamic sacred text at all, but I recalled the content had been dictated to the Prophet Muhammad by the Angel Gabriel who also made an appearance in the Christian Bible foretelling the births of John the Baptist and Jesus. Beyond the reincarnation theme, I found myself fascinated by Ehrlich's incorporation of the Iroquois concept of *Ondinnonk* — the most secret and innermost desire of the soul revealed in dreams — dreams that in Peter Proud's case were actually past life memories. All Ehrlich's threads combined to weave a fascinating tale, and the novel had held my attention well beyond the first chapter. I was curious now to see what happened to Proud, figuring the likely outcome would be he would discover exactly who he'd been and eventually face his murderer.

But I kept wondering what Jay meant when he said this book would explain a lot about us. As for me, I already knew the uncanny familiarity he and I shared had to be rooted in a soul connection beyond this lifetime. I didn't wear my metaphysical beliefs on my sleeve or talk about them very often, but they lived deep in my bones. For me, spirituality was personal, something between me and the Divine, not something to shove down other folks throats like almost every Christian sect I'd ever had the displeasure of getting to know.

I hadn't yet glimpsed where and when I'd known Jay before, but I'd figured it out with other people in my life, unsolicited pictures flashing in my mind during meditation. My most recent experience had been with my ex-boyfriend Kevin, who I'd watched carry a crate up the gangplank of a wooden sailing ship with tears in my eyes and a sleeping baby in my arms, never to return because he'd died of some fever off the coast of a smoking snow-capped island. How I "knew" whether any of that was really a past life wasn't quantifiable. When I saw that scene in my meditation, I'd felt the sadness and the pain of losing someone I deeply loved. But proving reincarnation didn't really matter to me. The way I figured it, what was already done was done. No changing it now. And although seeing the stories from a past lifetime might help explain how I felt about the person or unravel a strange dynamic, it was what we did now in this life that mattered.

A sudden flash on the horizon heralded the thunder, a rolling rumble that shook the apartment building. My living room lamps flickered briefly, then went dark as the transformers down the street hummed in protest. I collected candles from the kitchen drawer in the afternoon twilight and lit them, watching the glowing flames softly light the room. It wasn't quite enough bright enough for me to read comfortably, but it would be once I dug my battery-operated lantern out of the closet in my foyer.

So the question was: what had Jay thought of Ehrlich's book? Had he dreamed about a past life with me in it as he'd hinted? Or was he just learning about reincarnation and wondering what I thought? Snuggling back under my afghan on the couch, I sipped my now warm tea and closed my tired eyes.

Chapter Seven

Someone pounding on my door woke me a half hour later. "Jess, I know you're in there. I can see your car the parking lot."

I opened my apartment door a crack and peeked out into the darkness, which I immediately realized was a stupid thing to do because I did not have a chain lock. A tall dark haired man stood outside my door, holding a bedraggled bouquet of pale pink roses.

"I knew you were home," Kevin said, his voice sounding pleased. "So... hey... what's going on?"

"The power's out is what's going on. What are you doing here?" Perplexed, I studied Kevin's shadowed face. He looked down at his feet and shook his head.

"Ya gonna bust my balls? I know I deserve it, Jess. But I decided I had to at least try."

"Try what?" I rubbed the gritty sleep out of my eyes, too rummy to think straight quite yet. Either that or Kevin wasn't making any sense, which wouldn't be entirely surprising.

"You gonna invite me in?"

"Why not?" I opened the door wider and motioned him in, figuring it was the only way I'd get to the bottom of his unannounced visit.

"These are for you. I'm apologizing and shit. They probably need some water." Kevin shoved the wilting bouquet into my arms. He slipped off his black sneakers, then strode past me and took a leaping jump over the back of my couch. His bare feet landed smack dab on the center cushion, soon followed by his behind on the bounce. "Don't suppose you have a beer in your fridge?"

Same old Kevin, I thought, deciding to keep my irritation in check for the moment. I popped the top on a Corona and handed it to him, then opened one for myself and curled up into my old leather wingback chair on the opposite side of the coffee table.

One beer and fifteen minutes later I got the story: Kevin had come to apologize. More like plead for reconciliation. His mother and sisters had told him he was the biggest idiot in Sonoma County for letting me walk out of his life and, by his own admission, Kev thought they might be right. Would I please, please consider going out with him again. He promised he'd do better. Be more considerate. Besides, he had a good job now, driving for Nowalk Transportation, so he'd be able to afford to treat me the way I deserved to be treated. Like a queen...a beautiful queen. He was turning over a new leaf...

"Enough, already," I interrupted, finding a contrite and complimentary Kevin way out of character for the man I knew. I was now glad I had the foresight to choose the chair, rather than the couch, to ensure the conversation stayed a conversation rather than take any sudden romantic turns. "Why did we break up, Kev? Do you even remember?"

"Well, you broke up with me. I didn't break up with you." Kevin's voice sounded childishly adamant, as if breaking up had never entered his mind, which I knew was patently untrue because one of his sisters had hinted about it, but I chose to ignore that for the moment.

"Right. And why was that?" Fully aware I sounded like an impatient mother chastising a child, I was determined to make a point even if I had to pound it through the man's thick skull.

Kevin studied me through his irrationally gorgeous eyelashes, candlelight painting his gold-brown skin in russet shadow. Moving a few abalone shells and candles aside, he propped his long legs up on the coffee table and took a swig of beer.

"You used to always say I was disrespectful to women. But that's not true, Jess. I love women." He smiled his charming smile, showing a flash of white teeth.

"Okay. Stop right there. Look at your feet."

"What about them?"

"My coffee table is polished mahogany. Clearly not for feet. Never mind bare feet." I sounded like a bitch and I knew it, but somehow I couldn't seem to help it. I refused to let Kevin's piss-poor memory and blatant disregard for my possessions pass unnoticed. I wasn't going to put up with it.

"Sorry," he said, plunking his beer down onto the wood surface to quickly move said feet back to the floor and replace the shells and candle holders in their original positions.

"Better?"

"How many times have I asked you to use a coaster? We do not place wet glasses on a tabletop." Rapidly losing patience, I jumped up and grabbed a dishtowel from the kitchen counter and threw it onto the seat beside him as a hint. This inattention was classic Kevin, too stuck in his own world to care what got trampled as he buffaloed ahead to get whatever he decided he wanted.

"Right." Chagrined, Kevin grabbed a sandstone coaster from the holder and neatly mopped the water rings.

"I've told you this ten times, Kev. Maybe a hundred times. You don't care enough to listen. You can't do these simple things I ask you to do to respect my possessions. This..." I swished my hands at the table, "is the tip of the iceberg... it's the same way you don't respect me." Fidgeting in my chair, I tried to think of how to best express my thoughts. I wanted Kevin to understand. So he didn't keep making the same mistakes with women. At least that's what I told myself at the time.

Kevin looked a little bit hurt, but simply waited quietly for me to continue.

"It's the way you treat me. Like I'm just some kind of decorative appendage along for the ride. That I exist for your convenience. As if my priorities or opinions are unimportant. Immaterial. Not worth consideration." I paused, wracking my brain to come up with an example.

"I'm not like your friend's girlfriends..."

"You can say that again," Kevin huffed. "You're goddamn hot for one thing."

"This is so not about looks, Kev. It's about who I am. I'm in college *and* I work an office job. I have interests beyond hanging on someone's arm... not that Angelina and Jenny don't... Accckkkk... I don't know how to say this... I'm not saying I'm better than them in any fashion... I'm just wired with the drive to have an education and a career. To get somewhere. And somehow it always felt like you wished I was...simpler than I am. Like it would be easier for you if I didn't have other interests or school or a full-time job that take up my time. But I'm probably never be going to be like that. It all makes me wonder why you don't look for someone who fits your life better."

There. I'd said it. So why did my heart have this sick sinking feeling?

Kevin watched me from the couch. I couldn't quite read his expression in the semi darkness — something between frustration and humor, which made no sense at all. Finally he spoke.

"You think I don't know you're different. Hell yeah, I know it. And it's fucking great! You're smarter than anyone I know. You're not always after me to take you out to some fancy-schmancy place rather than play pool at the tavern with the guys. Or grabbing my at wallet for money. Or whining about why we have to watch football on Monday night. Hell, you even like football for chrissakes!"

Agitated, Kevin unfolded his long frame and stood. His thick hair brushed the top of his shoulders. He paced into the kitchen, opened the refrigerator, peered into the dark cavern, then closed it again. His nervousness permeated the room and I wondered what I'd hit on to make him suddenly so uncomfortable.

"What are you thinking, Kev?"

"I dunno." Kevin paced back into the living room and stood behind the couch. He shoved his hands into his jeans pockets as if to keep them from fluttering off.

"Yeah you do. Just say it." I sat up in my seat, more curious now. This fretfulness was unlike Kevin. Granted, he was used to getting what he wanted and I had repeatedly foiled him over the course of our relationship. If he thought a bouquet of withered roses and a few nice words were going to put everything back to the way we were, he was sadly mistaken. I'd tried not to think too much about reconciliation over the past few months. And since Kevin hadn't bothered to contact me since our disagreement up at the lake, I was beginning to think I'd never see him again. Of course, I'd been the one who'd screamed at him to never call me again. For once Kevin had done what I asked, which I'd taken as a sign — but who the hell knew what kind of sign. He'd either found someone else, was royally pissed off and determined to wait me out, or was glad we'd broken up and thought good riddance.

Being with Kev was like hanging onto a runaway train; you never knew whether you were going to crash and burn or roar triumphantly into the station to a round of applause. Kevin had jumped from one thing to another his entire life: jobs, roommates, trucks, get-rich-quick schemes. One girl to another too. Until me. We'd lasted a little over year — a tumultuous fabulous year that ended in an argument last September when I refused to put gas in his boat.

But that wasn't all the fight had been about. Not by a long shot.

Before we'd left town that Friday night for Lake Berryessa I'd asked Kev if we could come home early. I had a lot of reading for my fall classes and a short paper to write. I even considered staying home for the weekend, but Kev wouldn't hear of it. He suggested I bring my books and read on the boat, but I said it wasn't practical to study when we were towing water skiers at 30 miles an hour. So the compromise was for me to accompany him and we'd leave Sunday morning, which would give me Sunday afternoon and evening to catch up on school work. Except Kevin wasn't ready to leave Sunday morning: he wanted to go fishing instead. He left me at the campsite with the other guy's girlfriends while he went fishing with his buddies until almost noon, then he wanted to gas up the boat and take everyone on a final ski run before the drive home. When we pulled up at the dock to get gas, I refused to loan him the cash and reminded him I needed to get back to town to prepare for school on Monday. Kev called me a tight-wad bitch who had her stuck-up nose in a book half the damn time and what fun was that?

And there we had it. What Kevin really thought of me. Everyone heard it —Jimmy Cairnes and Terry Smithson, Kevin's grade school friends who now worked at Sonoma Diesel, and their girlfriends Jenny and Angelina Liu. Everyone saw how hurt I was. I swallowed my tears, grabbed my backpack, and told Kev we were over and to never ever call me again. I walked away without looking back. When I reached the main road, I stuck out my thumb and got a ride in the second car that passed.

Kevin hadn't come after me. Until now. Which suddenly struck me as being slightly suspicious. Why now and not Christmas or New Years?

"Just say it," I repeated, studying his face. "Otherwise, why are we here? It's been four months, Kev. I don't understand."

"OK. I just..." Kevin pushed his palms forward in a "stop" signal, then turned and headed toward the foyer, his tall frame moving with purpose. "I have something I gotta get in the Chevy..."

Before I knew it, he'd flung open the door and left the apartment. Cool air flooded into the living room as the wind whipped rain through the eucalyptus trees outside the walkway.

"Born in a barn?" I said, wondering what the hell Kevin was collecting from his beloved truck that he absolutely needed that very moment.

Minutes later I heard his bare feet pounding up the stairwell. He slid through the door and quietly shoved something small, square, and black into his pocket. Five steps later, he knelt by my chair. Dark hair fell into his eyes as he looked down at the carpet. I stared at him speechless, my mind turning slowly to comprehend exactly what was happening.

"I came here tonight because I love you, Jess. I always have. You know that."

Kevin paused to clear his throat. He looked up at me then, his eyes decidedly wet, and I felt how painful it was for him to say the words. Painful wasn't the right word... horridly uncomfortable was more accurate. Even after a four month absence, I knew this man's heart and mind like my own. I knew he absolutely meant what he said and the depth of his feelings; I could feel it emanating from his long lean body with an intensity I'd never felt before. Suddenly the end of our relationship in September made complete sense: Kevin had pushed my buttons so I'd be the one to break it off and walk away. Because breaking up was better than figuring out how to handle the feeling of loving someone so completely you'd come to their apartment on a Saturday night, kneel by their chair in the dark, and maybe propose something ridiculous like marriage after not seeing them for four months because you didn't want to live without them.

I could have been wrong about the marriage bit, but if that small black square was a ring box in his pocket as I suspected, then maybe I wasn't and I didn't really want to find out right that moment.

My mind felt scrambled. I couldn't let this happen. I didn't want this proposal — if that's what it was. Because I didn't think I could marry Kev, or anyone else for that matter. It just wasn't in my genes to be someone's wife for God sakes. Besides, there was this thing Jay and I had going and I'd have to tell Kev.... unless he already knew.

Maybe that's why Kevin was here now, because he thought I was moving on without him.

I had to think, goddamn it. Divert this conversation from where it seemed headed. But I didn't know what the hell to say to this beautiful man. So I said the first thing that came to mind. As the words tumbled out of my mouth, I realized they were true.

"I love you too, Kev." Collecting his idle hands in mine to prevent them from producing any small boxes from his jeans pocket, I smiled. "And I am absolutely starving. How about we find a place with lights and grab some dinner together?"

Breathing an unconscious sigh, Kevin smiled back at me. The moments seemed to move slowly, and I didn't know if he'd be able to let things stand without saying all that he'd come to say. Finally, he stood up, willingly to accept the diversion.. "You know, that sounds great." he said, shrugging the tension out of his shoulders. "Olivetti's? I know you like that Meatsa, but you like the garlic chicken too, right? Garlic-Lover's Gallina. Might be my favorite pizza of all time. But the Classic Chicago is a close second."

"The Gallina it is," I nodded, collecting my purse off the breakfast barstool. I breathed a silent sigh of relief, grateful the conversation had veered away from anything more serious for now — although I wouldn't be surprised if Kevin interpreted my willingness to have pizza with him a signal we were back together.

Truth was, since I'd been with Jay I'd stopped wondering if I'd ever consider reconciling with Kev. But there was one thing crystal clear in my mind, I was not —absolutely not — going to foot the dinner bill. It was high time Kevin made good on his promises about turning a new leaf and treating me better. Unfortunately that meant the Meatsa would have to wait until some other night and a dinner companion's whose stomach thought like mine.

"Are you reading this weird horror shit now?" Kevin held a copy of *The Reincarnation of Peter Proud* in his hand, his dark brows scrunched together. "I thought you hated this stuff."

"I usually do," I admitted, "but someone recommended it and it's actually not bad." I didn't want to explain Ehrlich's book or talk about reincarnation with Kev right that minute — or perhaps any minute. Kevin's Pomo grandparents had embraced Christianity lock, stock and barrel in an effort to appear more "white." To Kev, Native American spiritual beliefs like the Iroquois' *Ondinnonk* in Ehrlich's novel was just Indian voodoo and he couldn't care less.

"We going to Olivetti's or what?" As if on cue, my stomach growled.

Kevin heard the grumbling sound and smiled. "Let's get out of here." Tossing the paperback onto the couch, he grabbed me by the hand as if we were a couple again and the four months separation had never happened. I didn't have the heart to correct him, and part of me wasn't sure I wanted to.

Chapter Eight

"He knelt by your chair?" Rita's dark eyes widened in shock, two black buttons beneath the brim of a floppy red knit hat that had definitely seen better days. "The same Kevie Mac I used to know? Had he had too much firewater or something?"

The California rain pummeled the warehouse roof, creating a thunderous metallic roar. Rita and I stood beneath the entryway awning, Rita smoking a cigarette, me tapping my feet in a shallow puddle in rhythm to Anne Murray's classic country western hit *Could I Have This Dance?*. An image of Bud and Sissy dancing at Gilley's fluttered through my mind, as if looking for love in all the wrong places only happened between folks like John Travolta and Deborah Winger in the movies.

"Nope. He was totally sober. Said he loved me and was a fool to let me go." Yanking my long black leather coat closed at the front, I tried to quell my shivering. California or not, the day was downright cold.

"Hellfire. What did you do? Did he actually ask you to...?" Rita's voice trailed off before the word "marry." Despite her unequivocal appreciation of anything male, she didn't take to the idea of marriage any more than I did.

"No," I said, answering Rita's second question first. "I suggested we go out for dinner. Which sort of diverted the conversation." I gazed up at my friend. "Don't ask me whether we're back together. Kevin probably thinks we are, but I don't know. I just..."

"Jay," Rita said, her cranberry lips in a thin line. "You think Kev found out."

"Who knows?" I shrugged. "And if he did, so what? It made him jealous or something? Made him realize he was really losing me? Sometimes I have no idea what makes Kevin tick. But I have to admit, what happened Saturday night took me by surprise."

"Did you sleep with him?" As always, Rita cut right to the chase.

"God no! Not that he didn't have it in mind, but I didn't want to make him think everything was back to how it used to be. Because it isn't." I bit my lip and contemplated my next statement. "I've changed, Reets. I'm not the same girl who told Kevin to shove it last September. I'm not going to put up with the crap I did then. He needs to know that before... well, before we...you know..."

"Good," Rita said, her voice pleased. She pulled her rabbit lined leather gloves higher up to cover her thin wrists. "Kevie Mac needed to grow up. And maybe he has. But, then again, maybe he hasn't. Don't rush into anything."

"I don't plan to. But Kevin's impatient. You know that."

Earl Wyse stuck his bearded head outside the shop door, and peered across the parking lot. Spotting me beside Rita, he waved a summons. I waved back so he'd know his wayward office girl was on the way in just a minute.

"Yeah. But what I really want to know is what you want, Jess. Do you want Kev back? Or do you want something else? Someone else?" Rita looked at me out the side of her eyes, pretending a nonchalance I knew she didn't feel. Her question was loaded for bear, and the woman flat out knew it.

Essentially Reets was asking how I'd choose between Jay and Kevin. The answer was complicated, because Jay and I could never be together like other couples. He'd never leave his daughters without a father or Candy without a home. The man I'd grown to know and love was stuck in this 1950s paradigm of always doing the right thing — which I could never fault him for, but I knew how much grief his marriage had cost him. The bigger question was whether I was willing to wait it out until Jay's daughters were old enough that he felt like he could finally live his own life —

whenever that might be. None of this was new; Jay and I had discussed it and he was quite clear where his responsibilities lay.

Now it was my turn to get clear. Even though I knew he probably wouldn't ever do it, I'd been teetering on the verge of asking Jay to leave Candy because I couldn't stand the half-life of loving someone who I couldn't be with the way I wanted. I could barely admit that to myself, never mind to Rita. So instead I spoke the simple truth, knowing I had to remind myself things were what they were, and would probably never change.

"I can't have what I can't have, Reets. And I can't really have Jay. No matter how much we'd like it if things were different, they aren't." My throat suddenly felt tight, as if speaking the truth was that much more painful than simply knowing it. The sensation made my voice quiver, and as much as I hated the sound, I spoke anyway. "So all we have is today. Right now. No promises." I looked toward the foggy horizon, my eyes misty. Sugar-coating had never been my specialty, and I knew Rita would understand. "What I want doesn't really matter when it comes to any future with Jay. As for Kev, the door is open. I get to decide if I'm going to walk back through it or say good-bye for good. Because there's no middle ground with Kev — he's an all or nothing guy."

Chapter Nine

The next weekend I spent researching my Social Psyche paper. I absolutely had to finish it. I was behind on the project and had a midterm in Stats the following Monday. I badly needed to pull A's in those classes if I had any chance of getting accepted into grad school. Kevin tried to talk me into hanging out with him at the Riverrun tavern Saturday night, maybe play some darts, maybe stick around to hear the band, but I pleaded deadlines and refused the invitation. Interestingly, he took it in stride and said he totally understood, which surprised the hell out of me. I still hadn't firmly decided whether I wanted to fall into being Kev's girlfriend again. Part of me wanted to, part of me hesitated because choosing Kev undoubtedly meant giving up Jay.

I needed to talk to Jay and figure stuff out before I made any decisions. Yet I knew Jay wouldn't tell me not to go back to Kev. I was vacillating, procrastinating, putting off the conversations I didn't want to have. I was delaying the conversation with Kev because if we got back together, hands down he'd never stand for sharing his girlfriend with anyone. I was deferring the conversation with Jay because I didn't want to think about us ending. I also didn't trust that I wouldn't make a fool out of myself and ask him to leave Candy. But I knew things couldn't stay in this tense stasis. Something had to give and that something had to be me.

As Rita was fond of saying, it was a shit-or-get-off-the-pot moment. Somehow these decisions always seemed easy for other people; unfortunately, they weren't easy for me.

Sunday morning I settled onto my couch, coffee cup in hand, notebook in my lap, stacks of texts beside me on the floor. My Social Psyche paper was close to finished and I was feeling rather proud of my progress.

As soon as I thought the word "proud," I remembered Jay's book, *The Reincarnation of Peter Proud*. I'd stashed the tattered paperback on my nightstand, thinking I'd read it before bed, but then I hadn't finished it. Suddenly unable to focus on anything else, I retrieved the book and returned to the couch. I located my bookmark, poised now at the beginning of Part III.

Peter Proud had finally discovered his name in his previous life, read the 1946 obituary of his death by drowning, and obtained a smiling photograph of the man he used to be, a decorated World War II Marine. Now he was on his way to visit his own grave — kind of bizarre, but an interesting read. Ehrlich's novel built on Morey Bernstein's Bridey Murphy case, the possibility of "proving" reincarnation to Western non-believers by recalling specific historically traceable memories under hypnotic regression. The therapist in Ehrlich's novel, Hall Bentley, thought to make a fortune off Proud's story, not to mention shaking up the Christian status quo. I didn't need to be convinced of reincarnation myself, but I was reading the novel for Jay, so I finished it in a few hours. The conclusion struck me as inevitable — although somewhat a change from the "happily ever after" denouements many Western readers preferred. Death by drowning. Again.

The concept of repeated life patterns was not new to me. The Buddhists touched on this with the term karma, the endless wheel of births and deaths, the idea we repeat the same lessons with the same people until the debt is cleared. All with the idea that once we resolve what we need to resolve and evolve past attachment and desire, we reach enlightenment, no longer need to incarnate, and can transcend the physical plane. I'd also heard about the idea that groups of people chose to reincarnate together, to support each other's goals or work on a collective goal. It somehow made sense to me, and I didn't particularly care how or why. But with my Social Psychology paper research fresh in my mind, I wondered about how the intricacies of diverse family and cultural patterns intersected with individual life patterns and karma, and how to extricate one from the other, or even if you could.

Setting the novel aside, I wandered into the kitchen to make a chicken salad sandwich. Ehrlich's story also brought a tragic romantic element to the forefront. The power of love across lifetimes was one of my personal explanations for the phenomena many labeled "love at first sight." The cliché was one of those familiar Western literary tropes and the basis for thousands of songs, films, and poems, yet something many people personally experience. I'd experienced it to some degree with Kevin, but also oddly with Jay, the odd part being how I disliked him so much at first sight, and then — well the rest was our ongoing saga. I wondered whether Jay had experienced something like that with his wife or perhaps me. Recalling his request for me to read Ehrlich's novel with the promise it would explain a lot about us seemed to point in that direction. I had tried meditating on the subject of my past life with Jay, hoping to see the images of how and when we'd been together — like I'd seen with Kev — but so far, nothing.

The phone rang as I was chewing the first bite of chicken. I answered it, expecting Kevin's deep voice, but instead it was a woman.

"Hello, Jessica?" The woman's southern accent was soft, like a spring breeze across the prairie.

Figuring the caller was a telemarketer, I responded cold. but polite, thinking I'd hang up if I she didn't let me off the line gracefully. "Who's calling please?"

"This' Candace Green. I'm calling to speak to a Jessica Maneiro. Is she there?"

The bite of chicken lodged suddenly in my throat. I took a swig of water to wash it down, my mind rushing madly. Why the hell was Candy calling me? And did I even want to talk to her? Time seemed to slow as I considered my potential responses, most of them rude.

There was the standard "fuck off," the sly "wrong number," the bitchy "Candace who?," or the dumbfounded "what's up?" I settled on a version of "why not?". If Candy wanted to talk to me, I may as well hear what she had to say now and get it the hell over with. Otherwise I'd stew about it and imagine all kinds of shit and get wrapped around the axle thinking about it.

"This is Jess." I sat on the arm of my couch, trying nonchalant body language to mask my skyrocketing blood pressure.

"Hi Jess. This is Jay's wife, Candy." The woman paused, waiting for my acknowledgement.

"How can I help you Mrs. Green?" There was southern politeness for you, I thought, smirking to myself.

"Spare the sarcasm, please. This conversation is going to be short and to the point. I want you to stay away from my husband." Candy's words were clearly annunciated and remarkably calm.

Skipping any response to her directive regarding my sarcasm which would get us exactly nowhere, I quickly threw the ball back into her court. "I think you should be talking to Jay instead of me, Candy."

"I have talked to Jay. In fact, he knows I'm calling you right now. I'm telling you the same thing I told him. I want you out of our lives." Her voice sounded angry now. Petulant. A little girl who wanted what she wanted when she wanted it and barely hanging onto her temper.

The woman had nerve. No question. But I wasn't easily shooed away by tough girl talk. Wanting something didn't magically make it happen — for Candy or anyone else. The term soap opera fluttered through my brain. On the one hand, the situation felt inanely ridiculous, something right out of daytime TV, on the other, Candy's phone call was perhaps predictable. Pretty Candy had always been the one to step out on Jay first; it had never been the other way around. Now the shoe was on the other foot and she wanted Jay to herself again. Despite everything I knew, I suddenly felt sorry for the woman. Not that it changed my feelings about Jay one bit. But it made me sadly realize his situation was more sticky and complicated than I'd been wanting to see — which meant the possibility he'd leave her less likely even if I asked no matter how much he cared about me. Because Jay would always want to do the right thing for his family, regardless of the personal cost.

Swallowing the ache building in my throat, I wanted to slam the phone down. I didn't owe Candy anything. But meeting her anger with my own or spewing words I'd regret wouldn't help the situation. As I considered what I really wanted to say to Jay's wife, what came to mind was honesty and coolness for some reason. I didn't want Candace Green to think her call bothered me. I also didn't want to snap back with something defensive or bitchy that she could gossip about later with her girlfriends. Pettiness aside, this was a real woman, who for all her faults, meant something to a man I loved deeply and considered one of my best friends.

Taking a deep breath, I kept my own voice low and calm. "Well, I don't know about that, Candy. I don't think it's up to me. Again, I think that's something you and Jay should really be discussing between the two of you. But I want to thank you for calling and telling me how you feel."

There, I'd said exactly what I meant to say as kindly as I could say it. It probably didn't matter to anyone except me, but that was the point: I had to live with it.

"I'm telling you to stay out of my life, Jess." Candy's sweet voice was harsh now.

"Thanks for the call," I smiled into the receiver waiting for her to hang up on me, which she promptly did. I set the phone on the counter next to my sandwich.

My hands were still shaking five minutes later when I filled the tea kettle.

Shitfire. Sometimes truth really was stranger than fiction.

Chapter Ten

On Valentine's Day the following Tuesday I received two flower deliveries at the shop office. Earl Wyse studied the cut crystal vases on the Service Department counter, his long nose twitching as if he were about to sneeze.

"Two, Jess?" He frowned as if it were some type of sacrilege to receive two Valentine bouquets.

"What's it to ya, Earl?" I smiled.

"Who they from?" he asked, his gruff voice pitched like a teasing dad, then he snatched the card off the deep red roses and read the signature for himself. "Gotta be Kevin Mac," he guessed at the sloppy KM scribbled in black marker.

I raised my eyebrows and neither confirmed nor denied Earl's guess.

Without waiting for an invitation, he turned over the card beside the vase of gorgeous white calla lilies. "Now who the hell sends a girl flowers and then forgets to sign the card? A secret admirer?" The bearded man peered at me perplexed, then tapping his temple, he smiled. "Unless the girl sends flowers to herself."

I winked without bothering to correct him. Pleased as punch to have solved the office girl's two-bouquet mystery, Earl laughed his way through the swinging doors out into the shop.

At 6:00 pm, I wrapped up what I was working on and set the completed invoices on my desk to proof the following morning. I'd taken a "sick" day on Monday to study for my midterm and finish the Social Psych paper. Now that the deadlines were behind me, I felt I owed it to Earl to hold up my end of the table and crawl my way back to current on the billing. Keeping things current made Earl's numbers look good and he was a man who reveled in good numbers. On more than one occasion he'd made it clear I was substantially more proficient than the last "office girl" he'd hired — which was a fine arrangement for Earl and everyone else, including me.

The other quite deliberate reason I stayed late was to talk to Jay, who usually closed the shop every night. Although we typically went to dinner on Fridays, I thought I should at least thank him for the calla lilies (my favorite, sorry Kev...) and just maybe mention Sunday's conversation with Candy.

I'd told Rita about my unexpected phone call earlier over a meatloaf sandwich at Sal's Deli. As I expected, she'd flipped her perpetually-curly lid.

"Stay out of my life? As if little blonde Candy could snap her pretty fingers and everything would change just because she wants it to? Or else what? What's she gonna do, track you down at Olivetti's and shoot you?" Rita huffed and stuck a handful of potato chips in her month, then crunched them to smithereens, as if she were chewing pebbles.

"Not funny, Reets," I mumbled around a mouthful of sandwich.

"Well, for shit sakes. The bitch got what was coming to her. All those years she fucked around on Jay while he's IN the service. Then after he comes BACK, alive and whole and healthy, she takes up with some other soldier. Not to mention the entire hoo-ha with Dave. Which still may be going on, mind you. I can't believe her nerve." Rita furiously yanked her turquoise sweater into shape, exposing significantly more cleavage and the edges of a lacy black brassiere.

"What do you mean took up with someone after Jay was back? I thought they reconciled." Perplexed at Rita's version of Jay's history, I studied my friend's frown.

"The way I heard it, they did for a while, but you know their little girl Gracie isn't even Jay's. Not that he goes around advertising it, but Dave told me."

Leaning back in the booth, I shook my head. "Oh my God. I didn't know. Jay never said...."

"I don't know why he stays with her," Rita muttered, "Not many men would. Not even for their biological kids' sakes."

The two of us lapsed into a momentary silence. Jay Green was both my lover and my friend and my heart hurt to think about him willingly accepting another man's child as his own every damn night without complaint.

"I still don't get why Candy would call you," Rita said, shifting the conversation back on topic. "The slut needs to mind her own business. Did she think she'd intimidate you or something?"

"I don't know. I actually felt sorry for her at one point." I shrugged. "Thanked her for calling and telling me how she felt."

"I bet that chapped her perky behind," Rita chuckled. "Not many women would say 'thanks for sharing' in a situation like yours."

"Yeah, well, it sounded a lot nicer than fuck off."

Rita had laughed her ass off when I said that, but I knew she didn't think Candy's phone call was all that amusing. I didn't either. Since I hadn't seen Jay in two days, I was curious whether he even knew, whether Candy had lied about that little fact and he had no clue what she'd done.

Darkness still fell early in February, so by the time I donned my long black leather coat and made my way out into the shop, it was pitch dark outside. A cold wind swept through open truck bays, bringing the smell of imminent rain. My heels clacked on the concrete floor as I trudged toward the light in the tool room. Someone was sitting at the desk in there. I could see him moving in the shadows, and I figured that someone was Jay.

"Hey, stranger," I said, leaning against the door frame. "Long day?"

"Yeah. I gotta finish inventory this week. And the way these guys never put anything back where it belongs is enough to drive a man to drink." Jay smiled at me, his blue eyes crinkling at the edges.

The desk lamp painted his face in shadows, but I couldn't help noticing the dark circles, as if he hadn't slept well. Shifting from one side of the doorframe to the other, I studied his face. Jay wasn't just tired, he looked like he'd aged a decade.

"I wanted to thank you for the calla lilies. They're absolutely gorgeous." I smiled tentatively.

"I'm glad you like them, babe. You deserve gorgeous." Jay took a deep breath. "Good Lord, you deserve so much more than goregous, I...." Jay stopped and shook his brown curls. "I know Candy called you Sunday. I'm sorry."

"Yeah. That was a quite a surprise." I shrugged. "Don't suppose you could have really stopped her, but it might have been nice to have a warning."

"I know." Jay looked away, embarrassed. "I wish I could've... but everything happened so fast Sunday. Enough to make my goddamn head spin.

One minute we're singing the Lord's Prayer at church, the next we're fighting like snarling cats in the car on the way home."

"What happened?" I asked, curious now.

"All of a sudden, it's like a light switch goes off and Candy's screaming at me from the passenger seat. Called me a fucking prick of all damn things. And I'm yelling at her to shut her goddamn mouth because we don't talk that way in front of our kids. She keeps on ranting at me like I'd killed someone or something. The girls are wailing and crying in the back, thinking I've just done something terrible to their momma." He shook his head, closing his eyes briefly.

"It didn't end there. After we got home, she packed my suitcase and tossed it out on the lawn. Told the girls I was leaving. That I was in love with another woman and didn't want my family anymore. Screamed loud enough that the neighbors called the sheriff 'cause they thought I must be hittin' her or something. I was so stinkin' mad when the law showed up, they cuffed me and stuffed me in the back seat of the cop car, which made the girls more upset." Jay raked his fingers through his hair. "It was hell. Pure hell."

Shocked speechless, I simply stared at him. But he wasn't even close to done.

"Candy told me she was going to phone you, screamed it in front of the girls, calling you all kinds of rude names, but since the sheriff had taken me into custody about that time and then hauled me down to the station to give everyone a chance to cool off, I couldn't do a hell of a lot about it. I finally got a telephone call Sunday night and reached Dave who first went over to the house to make sure everything was OK with the kids, and then put in a good word for me with the sheriff. He gave me a lift home to collect my truck. I been stayin' at his place past few nights, swearing him to silence, but I figured that's only gonna last until the next time he sees Rita, which is probably right about now." Jay looked at his watch, then raised his eyes to look into mine.

"It was fucking bizarre, Jess. She never said or done anything like that before. Not that we'd never fought... but this time was totally over the top. Outer space. Mental shit. It wasn't like I'd kept us a secret from her... or like she'd never done the same. The whole thing was crazy."

"So, what are you going to do? I mean you can't go back."

Jay closed his eyes again and shook his head. There was a finality in his expression that made my heart sink. I leaned against the desk, afraid my knees would buckle. Somehow I felt like I knew what was coming and I didn't want to know it in the worst way.

"I wish...." He opened his eyes and reached for me, tears welling. "Dammit," he whispered, folding me into an embrace, "I wish that were true in the worst way, babe. But it ain't. Because there's more...." He pulled away then, a deliberate separation that felt somehow unnatural.

In the light from the shop desk lamp, I could see now that Jay Green looked like a beaten man. His expression held such misery and hopelessness, I nearly gasped aloud. I wiped the tears out of my own eyes with one hand, keeping my other on his arm in a futile attempt to keep him close. Because in that moment I felt him leaving me and everything in me didn't want him to go. The realization sent a crushing wave of sadness rushing through my torso. I didn't want to hear the next words he said.

I didn't want us to end.

Looking out the tool room door into the darkness, I saw the vision I'd been hoping to see for months — the shadows of the life we'd had together. A life on horseback running wild across an ocean of grass beneath a starry indigo sky, a life of shared love and work caring for a herd of gray-white palominos, a life with three dark haired children laughing, a life that ended all too early in an attack that left us torn and bleeding in the snow, our children sobbing with ropes around their small hands.

I turned back to Jay and realized he was speaking, his voice husky with emotion. "My whole life, I kept seeing this woman's face, like in a dream, but it felt more like a memory. I only seen it when I was camping out, sleeping under the stars. When you and me met, I knew it was you because my insides felt like I was falling off a cliff. And when I read that stupid book, I knew for sure. That we were, whatta ya call it. Reincarnated together? Fucking crazy, huh?"

Nodding, I found my voice. "Maybe not so crazy. Maybe meant to be."

"I wonder about that. I wonder about a God who would bring us together against all odds. Thousands of miles — maybe hundreds of years later —only to tear us apart again. Because with the news I got today, I got no choice."

"What do you mean 'no choice?'" I looked at Jay and saw the deep grief in his blue eyes. The grief was beyond exhaustion; it permeated his very bones. The feeling wormed its way into my chest, the heavy sickness in my heart another eerie warning. This would be a shared grief, and although I'd thought about what it might mean to go back to Kevin and break things off with Jay, I hadn't ever let myself feel what that might be like. I'd kept it at arm's length distance, a mental concept, not anything too terribly close, not anything that might hurt. At least not yet. But now it appeared I too might not have a choice.

"Candy called me here at work this afternoon. She's pregnant. Explains why she got so crazy emotional. Hormones and shit. " He looked at me and shrugged. "Swears it's mine. And, yes, I asked, dammit. I forgave her for Gracie eight years ago. Took that little girl as my own and never regretted it. But with all the rivers we've crossed since then,

I wasn't about to do that again. And selfishly, I have to say I hoped the child wasn't mine, because then maybe you and I..." His voice broke off for a moment, then he continued, finding strength from somewhere. "But I can't think about that anymore now."

Stunned, I blinked at him. "So, this means...."

"This means I go home," Jay said, nodding slightly. "Commit to being a husband and a father. Because I won't let any child of mine grow up a bastard. I just can't, Jess. I could never live with myself if I did."

Jay's arms folded around me and I sank against him. I put my head against his shoulder and listened to his strong heartbeat, wanting the moment to never end. Because as soon as I stepped away, I knew we would be over. For good.

"I'm sorry, Jess. I never intended to hurt you—"

"Don't be sorry. I'm not," I interrupted, my voice breaking. "Because you should never apologize for loving someone, no matter who they are. And we should never apologize for us. I won't and I hope you wouldn't either."

"No. You're right. And I didn't. I didn't apologize to Candy for loving you. Even though she wanted me to. Never will. Because these months of loving you have been the happiest in my life. And I'm gonna miss you so bad...."

Jay kissed me then and kept on kissing me. I'm not sure the tool room desk had ever been used in quite the way we used it that night. Or since, for that matter. When I left him an hour later, I held it together long enough to get in my car and exit the parking lot. I cried all the way home and most of the night, and, if I'm honest, most of the following week.

Jay's last words to me that night had been "I'll always love you."

Without reservations my response echoed his "And I'll always love you back..."

My belief that love was a veritable force of nature no one could limit included the capacity to fall in love with more than one person, a capacity I believed all humans had — whether they allowed themselves to experience it or not. Loving Jay never impeded my ability to love Kevin Mac. In fact, three months later when Kev asked me if I wanted children, I agreed to marry him and never regretted it.

Chapter Eleven

"We gotta go, Mom. Our reservations are at seven." Kyna peeked her head into the living room, brown-black eyes impatient, her purse hanging from her thin shoulder.

"All right already," I said, setting my book on the seat of my old leather wingback chair. "When did Olivetti's start requiring reservations for goodness sakes?"

"About ten years ago," Kyna sighed. "I'm driving by the way." My daughter collected her dad's old Chevy truck keys off the sideboard as I slid an indigo shawl with star patterns across my bare shoulders. Sonoma summer evenings still got chilly.

"Who's meeting us there, now? Aunt Kenzie couldn't come, but what about Gran?" I followed Kyna's long stride out to the driveway.

"Yup. Aunt Kyra is bringing Granny Mac. Then, Uncle Jim and Aunt Jenny with little Autumn, Uncle

Terry and his new girlfriend — I forget her name. Auntie Reets and Jenna for sure. Oh, and Zoe and Mattie and June of course."

"Right," I smiled, thinking of Kyna's posse of girlfriends. My daughter had the wonderful luck to be part of a fabulous group of girlfriends who were incredibly good-hearted. As for me, I had the wonderful luck to still be friends with Rita Garcia who had stood by my side through thick and thin and had practically been a second mother to Kyna the year Kevin Mac took sick, taking my sweet child on weekends to stay over with her daughter Jenna.

Sometimes it seemed like my all-too-short years with Kevin happened a lifetime ago. Other times it felt like it only yesterday. But the decade since Kev's death had been filled with the busyness of raising our lovely, willful girl child. Loneliness aside, they'd been good years for the most part. Kyna and I had been lucky to have such a close and caring extended family to help us weather the dark times.

Thanks to Kev's unfailing support in what he always called "my smarts," I'd finally left my Dum-Dum days behind and completed a Ph.D. in Psychology from UC Berkeley when Kyna was in pre-school. After years working as a Clinical Psychologist at Kaiser, last year I'd become a member of the Sonoma State Social Sciences faculty and was working on a book on social identity, how self-perceptions impact social interactions.

Revving up Kev's old Chevy pickup, Kyna shoved it into gear and backed out, taking care to check the side mirrors. On the way downtown, my thoughts strayed again to the man I'd married — only natural I suppose when a child celebrates a birthday and there's an empty seat at the table. Kev would have been so proud of his daughter, and he'd have loved to attend her seventeenth birthday party at Olivetti's. He'd have ordered the Garlic-Lovers Gallina while she and I shared a Meatsa Masterpiece and teased us the entire evening about our unrefined taste buds.

Olivetti's was packed, as usual. Our reserved table in the back corner had been boldly decorated with rainbow-colored balloons and streamers, courtesy of Kyna's friends and Auntie Rita. Amongst the whirlwind of greetings and ordering and toasting and gifting, I sensed a threshold looming. My daughter was beginning her senior year of high school in a month. She'd already applied to UC Berkeley and Stanford, and had the grades to make the cut if she wanted to study social sciences or business. She'd also queried UC Davis, not as prestigious, but since she was leaning toward the veterinary program, perhaps the better choice.

Next year at this time, Kyna would be packing to go to college and starting to plan her own life. I watched my daughter from beneath my eyelashes while I listened to Rita engage Kevin's mother in a conversation about pressure socks — my vivacious friend really could talk about anything. Kyna's thick dark hair was all Kevin's. Her golden skin, long lean body, wide smile, all Kev's too. But her eyes were deep and hazel, like mine, and her heart was a mirror image of my own humanitarianism, open and compassionate, filled with a deep desire to help others. I'd made a career out of helping others; Kyna would likely make a career out of it as well, but it looked as though her profession would lie in service to four-leggeds, rather than two-leggeds.

Collecting her empty glass, my daughter headed toward the open soda bar, her stunning waist-length hair flaring behind her as she dodged through the crowded restaurant. I watched a tall young man approach her, his golden brown curls noticeably long, his slightly cocky smile appreciative. As the young man spoke, Kyna tentatively looked in my direction. Then she shrugged and headed toward me, the young man following with dutiful determination. Grinning to myself, I surmised he'd asked for an introduction, and Kyna had acquiesced: he must either be someone special I didn't know about yet, or someone who wanted to be someone special.

I stood as my daughter approached and smiled as the handsome young man shook my hand. He reminded me of someone, but in that moment I couldn't place the resemblance. Then again, after all the clients and students I'd seen over the course of my career, everybody at some point reminded me of somebody else. Kyna pitched her voice above the crowd. I heard her say the name Jess and I nodded politely, thinking she'd introduced me. But then she laughed and simply said "Jess meet Jess."

We all laughed together then, the same name thing breaking the ice.

"Nice to meet you, ma'am." the young man said. "I asked your daughter to go out to a movie tonight and she told me I'd need to meet her mother before she went anywhere with me, so here I am."

"I see," I said, maintaining a straight face. "You're a brave man to meet the mom before the first date."

"Jess plays cornerback for the Santa Rosa Panthers," Kyna said, which immediately explained why she'd put him through the "meet the mom" formality, a test, so to speak. Jocks were typically not my daughter's type — although Rita and I had always told her "never say never" when it came to men. Kyna had undoubtedly played the "mom" card because she was still making up her mind whether she wanted to go out with a football player, not because my opinion would make a damn bit of difference whom she dated.

"I don't mind meeting you, ma'am. Not at all. My dad would say it was only right."

The young man met my eyes with an earnest honesty I found refreshing. His eyes were a striking sunrise blue, a shade I'd rarely seen in nearly two decades of public service work. The slightly southern accent surprised me enough to ask. "Did you move to Santa Rosa recently, Jess?"

"No ma'am. Lived here in Sonoma County my whole life. My parents were born 'n raised in Texas though, so I guess I come by a twang naturally."

Kyna stepped aside to hug her girlfriend Zoe good-bye, leaving Jess and I standing momentarily alone.

Trolling for a topic of conversation, I returned to his name. Our shared name. "So how'd you become a Jess. It's not all that common. Is your father's name Jess too?"

"Funny story, that. My mother gave me my first name, Brandon — her father's name. My father gave me my middle name, Jess, after a good friend of his. So, I'm a B.J. as my coach calls me. B.J. Green, just like my dad. I go by Jess with my friends 'cause I like it better. My dad goes by his middle name too. Not sure he ever used his first name his whole life. Folks call him Jay."

My heartbeat stuttered, causing me to startle. Kyna appeared at my side, eyes wide with concern. Tucking my long salt and pepper hair behind my ears, I smiled at her briefly to let her know all was well, then asked the question I knew I had to ask.

"Are your mom and dad here at the restaurant tonight?" I kept my eyes on Jess, refusing to look around like a frightened gazelle. I hadn't seen Jay Green in probably fifteen years, not since he'd accepted a field mechanic's position out of the

Caterpillar shop in Willits. At the time I figured it was his way of putting some distance between him and his home life, at least during the workweek. The thought of seeing him again made me suddenly blush, while the thought of seeing Candy kindled an unexpected tightness deep in my throat. Yet, seeing Jay's son, the resemblance so clear now, and hearing how the young man spoke about his father, I could tell the two were close.

My trepidation over seeing Candy dissipated into happiness for Jay and the blessing he'd had to raise this fine handsome son. Clearly, the young man was one hundred percent his father's — biologically and every other way that mattered — and I could only imagine the immense pride Jay must feel. Granted, the fact he'd named the child Jess was incredibly disarming. I hadn't known that teensy little fact. Thinking how Candy must have hated it, I smiled at the young man.

"Well, my mom's in Phoenix with my oldest sister who's having a baby next week. But my dad's coming in tonight from up Mendocino way to meet me for a Meatsa. And since he's the one buying, I'm just thumb-twiddlin' here waitin' on him." Jess turned toward the door, his eyes searching the crowd.

"You like the Meatsa?" Kyna laughed, her golden face alight.

"Best pizza on the planet," Jess smiled. "You too?"

"Absolutely. My mom and I both love it."

98

"My dad loves the Meatsa too, You know what they say... birds of a feather... 'Bout time! There he is coming through the door now. Hang tight while I grab him. I'd like to introduce you. " Jess looked at Kyna, his eyes searching her lovely face. "That is, if you don't mind...."

"Um. Sure." Kyna shrugged and watched Jess walk away, her eyes fixed on the view of his rather nice backside.

Behind me, Rita grabbed my elbow. "Who the hell is that kid? He looks exactly like—"

"Jay." I finished my friend's sentence. Then I locked eyes with a muscular man standing alone in the restaurant foyer. I stopped breathing then, stopped hearing the sound of the crowd, stopped wondering whether my daughter would ever break her own rule and date a football player.

I simply stood in the moment and waited for whatever was going to happen next.

Across the room, Jay's sky blue eyes studied me, his face shining with an incredulous joyful expression. Paying no attention whatsoever to the golden-haired son gesturing beside him, he didn't wave, didn't move, didn't blink, until the young man impatiently shook him by the shoulder. Then he nodded and smiled and I discovered I could breathe again.

Turning to Rita, I smiled too. "He looks exactly like Jay."

SONOMA SUMMERS

Never Say No To Love

Sonoma Summers Series (Book 2)

Jesse Devyn Crowe

PHOENIX PUBLICATIONS

ARDENVOIR, WA

In gratitude for the gift of children,

whether ours by blood or by fate...

Chapter One

The Northern California drizzle left the street artist pavilions dripping as the clouds began to clear. The Memorial Day weekend weather forecast promised eventual sun, which boded well for the Bay Area craftspeople who made their living selling handmade wares. Luckily I'd drawn a space for the weekend, so I'd rushed over from Santa Rosa early that morning to set up my booth, hoping to turn over some inventory and perhaps draw some portraits.

I positioned my placard on the awning, the swooping black lettering just above eye level. The sign read *Jack's House of Many Colors*, a play on the Jack London theme popular in Sonoma County. The name was also a way to maintain some androgyny in my side-business. On first glance, nobody would guess Jack was a woman, which was exactly how I liked it.

My easel rested at the front of the booth with a half-finished image of a winged fairy queen, pastels within easy reach of my stool. The tall racks behind me held some of my latest landscapes, watercolors of Sonoma Valley vineyards in bright summer sunshine, while the wide retail table beside me held bins with smaller matted prints in plastic sleeves. Vineyards weren't the only landscapes I painted in my spare time, but they were what sold, so I had a good selection of those, along with some Golden Gate Bridge and Sonoma Coast beach scenes. Tourists gravitated toward California cliché images, so I reluctantly complied, hoping to pad my savings account. One of these days I'd have enough to afford that trip to Paris and Rome to visit the art museums.

To advertise portraits, I always placed a large 3'x2' likeness of my cousin Rita in a full-length fuchsia cocktail dress holding a champagne glass on a stand at the front of the booth. Rita's warm brown hair was piled delicately on her head, curly tendrils framing her striking face. Due to the size and brilliant color, the piece captured a lot of attention, a few admirers even offering to purchase it. But my cousin had made it abundantly clear that although she'd allow me to draw it, I was damn sure not going to sell it to anyone but her.

Beside Rita, I placed some smaller children's images to show my range. You never knew when a family might drop by and commission portraits of their kids — granted, not my favorite subject, but admittedly one of my most lucrative.

As the sky cleared, the crowds swelled, tourists braving the puddles to browse the handmade crafts. Although the multi-colored booths resembled barely organized chaos, the Arts Commission managed the who, what, and where, instituting order to what used to be mayhem years ago. Thank goodness. Competition brings out the worst in people sometimes. I was glad they instituted the lottery process to make space allocation equitable for all the artists who wanted an opportunity to show in one of the most popular tourist locations in the world.

I pinned my long dark hair atop my head and sat before my easel, ready to meet and greet prospective customers and work a bit on the fairy queen. The morning passed quickly, a few print sales, but unfortunately no portraits. Pushing my disappointment aside, I positioned the first fairy queen on a small shelf facing the sidewalk and began another, a sister queen, adorned in ruby and apricot and gold, rather than the azure and amethyst that characterized the first. The delicate wings gleamed green-gold, a blur as if in motion. The verdant forest background held a simple pattern of dark green leaves and white jasmine, the flowering vine climbing a stone wall.

Around noon, a small blonde girl with freckles appeared by my side, eating a large vanilla ice cream cone.

"Hello," she said, peering around the easel.

"Hello. How are you today?" I smiled at the chubby round face.

"Whatcha drawing?" The child moved beside me to see the image. "Oh, it's a fairy!"" She reached one small hand with sticky fingers toward the easel.

"Let's not touch, okay?" I said, looking madly around for the girl's parents. "Where is your mom, sweetie? Did you bring her with you today?"

"No. She stayed home." The child's answer didn't help me any, so I pressed further.

"Is your daddy here or your auntie?" Grabbing a few paper towels, I wiped the child's gooey hands, then wrapped the ice cream cone so as to keep the sugary ooze contained.

"My daddy is here with my sister." The girl shrugged and took another voracious bite of ice cream, only to have the entire cone contents tumble first onto her yellow sun dress, then onto the pavement in my booth.

"OH," she cried, tears streaming down her freckled cheeks.

"It's okay," I said, quickly grabbing more paper towels to corral the melting goop to toss in the trash, then a few more to dab the dress.

"No," she wailed, "my daddy will be mad. He told me not to be messy."

"Everyone makes mistakes," I said, trying to make my voice sound soothing. "In fact, that same thing happened to me just yesterday." I pointed to a paint stain on my loose worn chambray shirt. "See look."

"That's a bad one," she assessed, tears forgotten for the moment.

"My name is Jacks," I said, holding out a semi-clean hand. "Could you tell me your name?"

"Hannah," she smiled. "Hannah Martin... But Jacks is a boy's name." She wrinkled her forehead in confusion. "You don't look like a boy."

Smiling, I shook my head. "No, you're right, I am definitely not a boy."

An elderly lady in a dark green sweater who couldn't help listening to our conversation selected one of my miniature matted vineyard scenes and handed me two twenty dollar bills. "She doesn't look like a boy to me either," she smiled down at the youngster.

"Thank you," I waved as the woman exited the booth.

"So Hannah, I'm worried your daddy is looking for you, thinking you are lost."

"I'm not lost," she said, very sure of herself. "I'm right here."

"How old are you?" I blurted, suddenly curious.

"Five," she said, holding out the appropriate number of fingers.

A traveling marimba band passed the booth, their music making further conversation impossible for a few moments. Hannah watched the musicians with wide eyes, her shoulders tipping back and forth. I smiled at her subdued dancing, then stood and said. "You gotta put some hips into it, girl!"

Stepping in front of the booth, I demonstrated, holding my arms out to the side, hands tipped, hips and shoulders rolling to the rhythm as my feet moved side-to-side on the pavement. "Come on, give it a try."

Hannah began imitating me, her rosy cheeks grinning. Her long blonde hair swayed out and back as she eventually found the beat. A few tourists stopped and watched us dance together, enjoying the show. I took Hannah by the hand and twirled her around, until she became dizzy and began giggling so hard I feared she'd careen into one of my tables.

"Okay, enough for now, " I said, pinning her by the shoulders to halt her spin. "So... where did you leave your daddy and sister? "

"Over there," she pointed to the right, shrugging.

"I think we may need to find a policeman. He can help you find your daddy." I grabbed my purse, then signaled to the neighboring vendor. Keeping an eye on an adjacent booth was a courtesy we performed for each other whenever one of us needed to step away.

"No, Jacks. Please." Hannah turned her back to me, her hands covering her eyes. "I want to stay here with you."

What the hell was I supposed to do now?

"Your daddy must be so worried about you Hannah. I just know it. We need to find him. It'll be okay. Come on." I reached for her hand and after a moment's hesitation she allowed me to take it. We moved out into the crowd, but had only taken a few steps when I heard a man's desperate shout.

"Hannah! Hannah, where are you, honey?"

"She's here," I yelled back. "We're at Jack's, the pastel booth."

A moment later I caught sight of a handsome man dodging through the crowd, his eyes frantically searching every booth, another small blonde girl in tow. "Where's Jack's?" I heard him ask the pottery vendor. Finally he saw the two of us, swung the second child up to his chest, and rushed toward me.

"Thank God," the dark-haired man sputtered, his gray eyes relieved. "Thank God you found her." He set the smaller child down and squatted to hug Hannah. "I was so worried, punkin. What happened?"

"I dunno," the five-year old said, her eyes downcast. "I went to hear the guitar men playing and then I found Jacks."

"You found Jack's, yes. This nice lady was helping you." He peered up at me. "I can't thank you enough, I—"

"No," Hannah interrupted. She reached out her hand and prodded my leg. "I found Jacks."

"Jacks. That's me." I smiled at the handsome man squatting in front of me.

"I see. You found Jacks. Good job, baby."

The man stood then, his lithe frame moving with a dancer's balanced grace. "Carl Martin," he said, but did not offer his manicured hand. "I want to thank you for your time and trouble, Miss Jacks." He removed his wallet from his back pants pocket and flipped through the bills until he came to the hundreds. Grabbing one hundred, then a second, he pushed the money toward me.

I stared at the cash in disbelief, then gazed up at him. "That's really unnecessary."

Nodding, he removed an additional hundred from the wallet. "I insist. And not a word to *anyone* about Hannah getting lost today." He nudged the money in the direction of my hand still resting beside my leg.

I squinted at him, trying to figure out his gig. Carl Martin was quite an attractive man, but treating me as if I were some servant looking for a payout was blatantly rude. I wanted absolutely nothing to do with him. Or his money.

Sighing impatiently, he lowered his voice. "I am buying your silence, Miss Jacks. I don't need this incident getting any publicity. If the tabloids pick it up..." His voice sounded suddenly wretched, his eyes darting in all directions. "I could lose visitation with my children...."

112

Head shaking, I took one giant step backward. "Keep your money, Mr. Martin. I don't expect to be paid for a simple act of kindness."

"Then perhaps we could purchase something from you. One of these paintings?" Carl peered around, studying my small gallery booth.

In the neighborhood where I grew up, a payoff was a payoff, regardless of the trappings. I wasn't interested. I refused to accept money for helping a lost child. Grabbing my red Closed sign, I plunked it on my table. "Unfortunately, I'm closed , Mr. Martin."

I smiled at Carl's freckled blonde daughters. "Nice to meet you, Hannah. You guys have a nice day." What I wanted to say to the man was "fuck off," but I wouldn't curse in front of his children. Instead I walked away. It was the only way I could think of to get rid of the rich jackass.

Chapter Two

The following day the weather cleared and business absolutely boomed. I sold one of my larger vineyard landscapes and more prints, and kept busy most of the day with portraits. The public attention devoted to an artist at work always astounded me. Unfortunately when the artist was me, I couldn't pay too much attention to the crowd. But after I was done, I would look around at the smiling faces and feel warm inside. Of course, I typically received glowing comments and more interested buyers afterwards as well, which was good for my pocketbook.

My last portrait of the afternoon was a lovely nine year-old Japanese child with jet-black hair. The girl's eyes were light blue, something I'd rarely seen. She sat quite still for the portrait, holding the white-blue peony her mother selected. The blues were a near match, and in the drawing I made it so, the vibrancy a contrast to her white dress and long dark hair. I always kept a bucket of flowers at my feet for portraits, often asking a girl to select one herself. I thought of it as a representation of who they were becoming. For young boys, I kept a few carved wooden toys, a train and a horse, along with a baseball mitt and small football. Older children rarely elected to hold anything, but I didn't mind because by about age 12 their clothing and jewelry choices were more characterizing and I worked with that instead.

As I wrapped the girl's portrait in brown Kraft paper, I noticed Carl Martin standing alone behind the group that had gathered to watch me work. Clad in Ray-Ban sunglasses and a deep purple golf shirt, I watched him shift anxiously from foot-to-foot. His polished Italian loafers gleamed blue-black beneath his form-fitting jeans as he approached me with a determined expression. I didn't particularly want to speak to the man again, but I didn't have much choice because my booth held a handful of interested customers perusing my prints and asking questions.

"Good afternoon, Miss Jacks," Carl said, removing his sunglasses in the shade of my booth.

"How can I help you today, Mr. Martin?" I raised my eyebrows, all business, hoping he did not want to revisit the prior day's conversation, because I absolutely would not accept the man's payoff.

The gray eyes studied me, hesitant, and I realized he was quite nervous. "I came to apologize for my horrid behavior yesterday. I —"

"Jackie, there's no price on these fairy queen pieces. Are they for sale?"

I turned to the woman standing beside my easel who had spoken. "I haven't priced them yet, Leyla. I thought I'd do a trio. Are you interested?"

"Absolutely. This is new work for you. More like fantasy portraits, yes? I love them. And so will my granddaughters." Leyla smiled, warm appreciation in her voice. Then her eyes sharpened and she stepped closer. "Are you by chance Carl Jacobs Martin?" she asked, studying the lithe man beside me.

"I am," smiled Carl. "And you are?"

"Leyla Abrams. Pleased to meet you." The older woman blushed with pleasure. "You are interested in our Ms. Jacqueline Carmichael's work today?"

"Indeed," Carl said. "My daughters were here yesterday and became positively smitten with those same fairy queen portraits. My Hannah has spoken of nothing else since."

Before my eyes, Carl transformed from nervous and hesitant to smooth and magnanimous, as if he'd somehow flipped a switch. I stared at him, perplexed. Who was this man? A celebrity I didn't recognize or something?

"I'd hoped to speak with Ms. Carmichael," — he spoke my name correctly and gazed pointedly

116

at me — "about a commission." Carl nodded at Leyla as if it were her idea.

"How exciting!" Leyla gushed. "You can do no better than Jackie, Mr. Martin. I will leave you two alone. Unless perhaps you might...." Leyla produced a pen out of her pocketbook and what looked like an old grocery list.

"Of course," Carl agreed, gripping the pen between his fingers and signing the paper scrap with a flourish.

By then my remaining customers had completed their purchases and followed Leyla out of the booth, leaving Carl and I to our conversation. Taking a deep breath, I piled the receipts quickly in my cash box. "You were saying something about horrid behavior?" I turned to the man beside me, my dark unpainted eyebrows raised.

"Yes, I—" Carl Martin stuttered, nervous now again. The early evening hour had driven many patrons to the Sonoma Valley's excellent restaurants. Street music played a merry accompaniment to the sound of distant traffic. We were nearly alone on the sidewalk now, with the exception of the vendors in the booth beside me packing up for the day. I needed to do the same, but first I wanted the business with Carl Martin over.

"Wait. First tell me who you are." My curiosity had gotten the better of me. I had to know.

"I am currently an agent for some rather popular people in the sports entertainment industry ," he shrugged. "Some people, like your Leyla, recognize me. Most others wouldn't."

"I see," I nodded. "So why are you here in my booth today, Carl?"

"As I was saying, I wanted to apologize for my horrid behavior when Hannah ran off on me. I was an ass. A frantic ass. Worried something terrible might have happened to her. And then I was so relieved she was found and cared for.... She told me how you cleaned up her ice cream and how you danced together and... really she's spoken of nothing else since. I wasn't joking about the fairy queen pictures earlier. Yesterday I became so concerned that she'd tell her mother about getting lost — about me losing her, that is — and the incident would be used as ammunition against me in our rather nasty custody battle." Carl threw his hands in the air and shook his head.

"I don't know why I'm telling you all this. But I want you to understand why I tried to give you that money. Idiotic as it seemed, it was out of sheer fear that the fact I'd lost my child at a street fair would somehow get out and the consequences...I don't blame you for not taking the money. I respect that. More than you know."

I thought he was finally done then and took a breath to respond, but he waved his hand as if to say "not yet" and continued.

"You see, I love my daughters, Miss Jacks... I mean Ms. Carmichael...." Carl paused for breath. "I

118

can't lose them. I just... can't. So I've come here today to apologize. And to start over...."

Sticking out his manicured hand, he smiled a wan smile. "Hello, I'm Carl Martin. Pleased to meet you, Ms. Carmichael."

"Thank you, Carl," I said, eyeing his outstretched hand before grasping it. "I accept your apology. As for all the rest, I've just seen you don personalities like changing suit jackets, so I don't know what to believe." I gazed up into his eyes expecting to find the smooth, suave, performer looking back at me. His touch felt warm, but it was his eyes that radiated an uncanny heat that made him all the more handsome. He brought my hand to his soft lips in a gentlemanly fashion that somehow made my toes tingle, his eyes never leaving mine.

"Please believe me when I say I am being entirely sincere with you, Jacqueline." He covered my hand with his free one, cocooning me in his warmth. "You are as refreshingly honest as you are beautiful. And talented." Carl tipped his chin toward my work on display. "After you unexpectedly left yesterday, the girls and I toured your booth. Is this your living? Selling paintings? Drawing portraits?"

"No. I, uh, work weekdays for a graphics arts firm in Santa Rosa. This is just a weekend gig. Whenever my number is drawn in the Arts Commission lottery." I slowly extricated my hand from his, trying not to show my growing

119

discomfort. Yesterday I'd thought the man was a rich prig; today I was seeing a different person, one who seemed so... human. A father who didn't want to lose his daughters. A man willing to apologize for being an ass. A gray-eyed charmer who kissed women appreciatively on the hand with his soft lips and made their toes tingle.

Carl cleared his throat. "This may seem rather forward, but would you join me for dinner tonight, Jacqueline?"

"Thank you, but no. I'm already busy," I lied, feeling somewhat taken aback by his disarming directness and the impromptu invitation. It made no sense that he would ask me out and I felt suddenly uncomfortable at being the subject of his undivided attention. I turned away and began the task of packing up the booth.

"Consider dinner part of my apology. Consider it also a business opportunity. I have a number of clients who occasionally require a graphic artist to help them brand their side-businesses. I think your work may be a match for a few of my lady clients."

I shook my head, trying to shake loose the cobwebs. The man was so intense, a Jekyll/Hyde with personal and business personas he rotated with disarming speed.

"I'll think about it," I decided, putting him off. "I have some commissions lined up already, so I'm not sure that's something I can take on right now."

"May I call you next week to set up a meeting?" He grabbed one of my business cards from the table.

"Sure," I sighed, too tired to argue with him. The man was persistent, and if there was any truth to the potential business he might send my way, I definitely should consider it. Besides, what could it hurt to take a meeting?

"And...may I purchase one of the fairy queen paintings for Hannah? I promised her I would ask if they were for sale." Carl's voice sounded both sincere and apologetic.

"Do you ever slow down?" I turned back toward him, a cardboard box of prints in my arms.

"Here, let me help you," Carl said, immediately grabbing the box.

"No," I said, wrestling the box of prints away from him. "I'm quite capable, Mr. Martin. My friend will be here shortly to help me load everything up and I need get things ready."

"Is this a special friend, by chance?"

"None of your business!" I sputtered, incredulous at the man's relentless questioning.

Carl nodded, looking mildly sheepish. "Of course. I—I apologize again, Ms. Carmichael."

Our eyes met over the box in my arms. The waning sun had turned his gray irises to a very light shade of violet. Wisteria to be exact. I knew it was a trick of the light, the deep purple shirt somehow influencing how my brain perceived the gray, but it was striking nonetheless, making me study the man's handsome face. The elegant nose, the smooth skin, the curving lips, the gentle jaw line. I reluctantly pulled my attention away and returned to the business at hand.

"So, one of the fairy queen pictures for Hannah?"

"Please. If you are willing to part with it."

"For Hannah, I will," I decided, digging my camera out of my bag. "Which one were you thinking?" I didn't recall whether Hannah had a favorite or whether her father would know the difference.

"Oh, the red one," Carl smiled. "Thank you."

"Let me photograph it first, and then I'll wrap it for you."

"Wonderful. Perhaps... you'd also consent to selling the purple one as well? For my younger daughter, Eloise?"

"You are an unrelenting persistent booger, Mr. Carl Jacobs Martin," I laughed, placing the two fairy queens side-by-side on my table.

"I am," Carl admitted. "People rarely say no to me for some reason. I've been told I wear them down, a quality that has served me mostly well."

I began wrapping the fairy portraits, considering the "mostly well" caveat, but decided not to pursue further conversation. Best that Carl Jacobs Martin be on his way and me on mine. I was a California street vendor in Birkenstock sandals, faded overalls, and a stained chambray shirt; he was a rich entertainment executive. We moved in different universes, different classes. People liked to think America was a classless society, but I knew better. Business interests aside, I was not part of Carl's world and never would be, and I knew it.

"Here you go," I smiled, handing the brown paper package to him.

"There is the matter of the price?" Carl reminded me, extricating his wallet from his back pants pocket again.

"Five dollars," I said, watching his dark eyebrows crick over the gray-violet eyes.

"That's not nearly...." He shook his head, removing a hundred dollar bill from his wallet.

"Let's not haggle over this," I said, holding my hand in front of me as a stop sign.

"No, let's not." Carl's insisted. "Please let me pay you what they are worth."

"Please let me gift the fairy queen to Hannah," I countered, knowing I'd invoked an unfair advantage by mentioning his daughter's name.

"You are incorrigible, Jacqueline!" Carl pursed his lips, his eyes a cloudy gray now.

"I am," I smiled sweetly.

"Fine," Carl huffed. "I only have twenties." He slapped a bill on the table, his expression irritated. "Good day, Ms. Carmichael." He hesitated as he turned, as if not wanting to go, but having no excuse to stay.

"Good day, Mr. Martin." I watched him walk down the sidewalk, the lean, muscled physique moving with a smooth athletic grace. Carl Jacobs

Martin was a very handsome man, a man who undoubtedly had a line of Hollywood starlets waiting at his door. Although he *had* asked me to dinner and taken my card, I'd probably never see him again, except for perhaps on the entertainment news if I ever bothered to watch it.

So, why did the thought make me feel so misty-eyed?

Chapter Three

Carl waited exactly the requisite three polite days to call. Three days where I'd wondered whether I was a crazy person for thinking there had been *something* between us. Something that had captured his interest sufficiently to lead to a future meeting — most likely business, rather than pleasure, of course. At a minimum, an interview with a portfolio presentation. His message had sounded somewhat breathless: Vicente's Bistro, 8pm, Saturday night, he'd send a car.

Yes, Carl Jacobs Martin had piqued my interest, and if our encounter took a turn away from business toward the pleasurable side of the tracks and I had an opportunity to kiss those soft lips, I decided I was not above taking advantage of it. Not at all.

Since Jim and I had separated a year ago, I'd been rather hesitant when it came to men. Appreciative and attracted, of course, but cautious.

Not that the separation hadn't been amicable; Jim was probably still my best friend, except for my cousin Rita. He and I had moved out to California together from New York after we graduated high school and built a life in Santa Rosa where he had friends. I was a good match for his bohemian musician lifestyle and fit in well with his California musician crowd. The group's philosophical and metaphysical interests — along with their liberal politics — kept our late night discussions lively. Not that I minded; the band members and their girlfriends were a fascinating group, notwithstanding their penchant for partying every night. Jim had always been supportive of my art, my number one fan, going to great lengths to help me with setting up and tearing down the booth on weekends when I was lucky enough to draw a spot at one of the local street markets. But when his interest in me waned, I suspected it had more to do with our handsome neighbor Timothy than anything between us. When Timothy moved in a month after I moved out , I embraced them as a couple.

Can't fight the inevitable. We love who we love.

Recalling Jim's lithe muscled frame, I marveled over how my old lover was a blue-collar mirror image of Carl Jacobs Martin.

No, we really can't help our attractions, can we?

Vicente's Bistro was upscale Sonoma Valley dining. Italian and expensive — not to mention delicious. Saturday evening I decided to dress for the restaurant, rather than a business meeting. My amethyst satin cocktail dress was straight 1950's with a form-fitting bosom, cinched waist, and dramatic flared skirt. The halter top straps left my shoulders bare, the top snug across my breasts, showing some tasteful cleavage. With matching purple eye shadow, a pearl choker necklace, and my dark hair long and loose, I didn't look half bad. Gazing at my reflection in the full length mirror in my bedroom, I smiled, recalling Rita's comments when she'd first seen me in the dress last year clubbing in New York. *Those boobs are your secret weapon, Jacks. Why would anyone look at the rest of us waifs when they can feast their eyes on you.*

I didn't especially agree with her — because my cousin was rather attractive in her own right. But I had to admit she was right about one thing: the boobs were definitely noticeable. Hopefully Carl would be paying attention.

At 8 pm exactly, the black town car pulled up in front of my apartment building. Donning a black lace shawl, I picked up the oversize portfolio case, and trundled down the stairs in my ankle strap heels. The driver opened the door and ushered me inside, taking great care to place my cumbersome bag on the wide seat beside me, then repeated the ritual again in reverse order outside the restaurant.

Vicente's was busy as usual for a Saturday night. I paused by the mahogany host podium. "Name please, miss?" The dark-haired maitre de smiled, his eyes firmly fixed on my face, rather than my outfit.

"Jacqueline Carmichael. I'm meeting Carl Martin." I returned the smile and shifted the large portfolio to my other hand.

"Of course. Allow me, miss." The man held out his hand to carry my case.

"Thank you," I demurred.

"Right this way, please." The host led me through the restaurant toward a half-round booth at the back where Carl waited, a bottle of champagne in an ice bucket on a stand to the side. As we approached, Carl raised his head briefly, looked right through me, then return his gaze to the paperwork in front of him.

In a flash, my brain fled down a twisty trail of doubt. Was I that unmemorable? Or simply unimportant? Should I have even accepted this man's invitation? Perhaps I could simply keep walking and find the back door to the alley. Embarrassed, I felt myself blushing as we arrived at the table.

"Ms. Carmichael, sir," the maitre de announced, placing my portfolio gently beside my seat, then quickly scurrying off.

Pausing awkwardly beside the table, I realized Carl was now standing. Smiling politely, I looked up into his face.

"Jacqueline, I..." he stuttered, his cheeks flushing beneath his tan. His hands unconsciously cupped my elbows, gray eyes smiling with what I could only interpret as surprise. "You are... absolutely stunning. Please... sit."

I sat as invited, trying to retain what grace I could in this odd situation, and folded the shawl beside me on the seat.

A moment later, Carl collected my hand and brought it to his lips, the motion graceful and gentlemanly and undoubtedly sensual — perhaps more than he realized. As I watched his soft lips touch my skin, I felt the sensation zipping up my arm, down my side, into my thighs and out my toes. It took everything I had not to wiggle in my seat.

"I must apologize," he said, sitting across from me. "It seems I am doing that a lot this week... I did not recognize you at first glance. You are... very different... than the artist in baggy overalls I remember." His gray eyes studied my long curled hair and bare shoulders.

"You mean I clean up good," I laughed, retrieving my hand from his grip.

"Beyond good," Carl said, his voice insistent. "You're hands down one of the most gorgeous women I have ever had the pleasure of dining with... probably ever."

I looked at him and laughed again, certain he'd switched hats to the suave performer for my benefit.

"You don't believe me?" he said, incredulous and slightly petulant. He cocked his handsome head, smiling.

Shaking my head, I opened my portfolio. "As we discussed, I've brought some of my work to show you tonight."

"Please." Carl graciously allowed me to change the subject, turning his full attention to my presentation. I began with small prints of some of the cliché California images he'd seen in my booth.

As we talked, the waiter opened the champagne and filled our glasses.

"Lasagna sound all right?" Carl asked.

"Fabulous," I nodded, then arranged some of my current corporate graphic arts work for his inspection.

"Cheers," we both said, absently clinking crystal. Then I returned to the business at hand, describing some of my recent projects with local wineries, small businesses trying to make a name for themselves and wanting unique eye-catching labels to draw consumer interest.

Dinner arrived and we ate the delicious meal, our animated conversation consuming our attention. The overlap in our roles as agent and designer became more apparent the longer we talked. Carl explained how many athletes and entertainers worked on packaging and marketing themselves, from their physical appearance and wardrobe, to the roles they solicited and accepted, to the public appearances they chose to make, to the adjunct businesses they invested in. It was fascinating how he served as an advisor of sorts, not only a contract negotiator.

"But I am not actually an artist," he clarified. "I know what works, what sells. When I see it. But I couldn't tell you what that is. I couldn't make it up out of thin air."

Vicente's was winding down for the night, the last few patrons departing as the wait staff began stripping tables.

"We should go," I said, trying to hide my disappointment. "They're preparing to close." I had enjoyed Carl more than I ever imagined I would and didn't want the evening to end. Perhaps it didn't need to; if he wanted to continue the conversation, I could brave rejection and invite him up to my apartment for a nightcap.

"Of course," Carl said, suddenly aware of the hour. "I've been so focused on our conversation, I lost track of the time."

"Come," he said, taking my hand. "I'll drive you home."

Nodding, I stood, my body quite close to his, my breasts nearly touching his torso. He did not step away as I expected he might, but drew my hand to his chest. His heartbeat thrummed through his clothing, a mirroring dance of the blood rushing in my own veins. The gray eyes gleamed blue tonight in the muted restaurant lighting, a reflection of the tailored navy pin-striped suit that graced his lean muscled frame.

131

I tipped my face slightly to look up at him; in heels I was nearly his height. Before I knew it, his lips found mine, as soft and gentle as I imagined. Slow at first, then more insistent and passionate, until he abruptly broke away.

"I know I shouldn't have done that, Jacqueline." Carl stepped away from me and collected my portfolio with his free hand, keeping my other cocooned in his warmth. "But I enjoyed it too much to apologize." Smiling, he shrugged. "I hope you won't slap me across the cheek or anything dramatic, but, then again, I'd probably deserve it for the thoughts I've been thinking all evening. "Shall we go?"

Chapter Four

Pleasantly stunned by the unexpected kiss, I followed him out of the restaurant to the sleek black car. We sat side-by-side in silence on the long leather seat, until the driver put the vehicle in gear. Then, composed once again, I turned to him. "What thoughts?" I asked, taking his hand in mine and bringing it to my lips. I kissed his knuckles softly, peering up at him from beneath my dark eyelashes.

"Oh... luscious thoughts. Male thoughts. Things I should not have been thinking at a business meeting with a female colleague." Carl stared at his hand against my lips. "And, ah, what you are doing there right now is not making it any easier for me to set those thoughts aside."

"No?"

"Absolutely not."

"Say more," I said, drawing his hand onto my satin leg and massaging it with my fingers.

"I couldn't," Carl laughed, primly aghast. "You are incorrigible, Jacqueline. Lovely and quite sexy, you know. Fabulous pair of breasts and all that. But horribly incorrigible. I have never in my entire life kissed a colleague after a dinner meeting. In public no less."

"Never?" I moved my free hand to his face, my thumb tracing his lips. "That's a shame, because you have quite delectable lips, Mr. Martin. I wouldn't mind trying them again. Perhaps over a nightcap, if you want to come up to my place...." I gazed at him pointedly, my message clear.

Eyes suddenly wide, Carl corralled my hands safely in his and set them gently on my lap. I could tell he was second-guessing himself, reconsidering his actions. "I don't think that's a good idea."

In the darkness of the limousine, I sensed his immediate discomfort and guessed his reaction was about more than the blurred roles of business colleague or potential romantic date. I took a stab at the obvious.

"Are you still in love with your wife?"

"Oh God, no." Carl barked a laugh. "I haven't lived with *or* kissed Victoria in years. She lost interest in me after Eloise was born and I guess that's... how it goes sometimes. With women, that is..."

"Oh?" I said, trying to piece together what he meant.

134

"I was determined to stay faithful to my marriage, even though my wife and I weren't sleeping together. After a year of seeing a couples therapist — God knows I tried — I decided to file for separation. It didn't seem like there was anything left in our marriage worth saving, and I did not want us to be so miserable any more. Victoria had changed so much since we got married, and was so unhappy. Honestly, since my marriage fell apart, I haven't met any women who piqued my interest."

"Do you prefer men?" I asked, my stomach sinking at the thought I'd chosen another attractive man like Jim who wasn't terribly into women. I transferred my gaze out the window, watching the city lights blur past.

"No, although at times I wished I swung that way. It might have been easier to stay married," Carl sniffed. "Until tonight I thought... well to be honest I tried not to think about it. In our family, marriage means forever — but apparently not for me. My parents were terribly devastated by the news of my separation and worried about my daughters growing up without a father, as if I was abandoning them...." He pointedly cleared his throat. "Well, this is a rather personal topic of conversation for a business meeting."

Taking a deep breath, he continued, "I started this, I might was well finish it. Jacqueline, I have spent a most wonderful evening with you...."

135

Here it comes, I thought, the *you're nice, but not my type* or *you're pretty, but...* fill in the blank. Thanks, but no thanks. What was it with my taste in men?

"A most wonderful evening." Carl repeated, "I enjoyed the meal, the conversation, the marvelous company," he nodded at me, his lips in a smile. "I thought your portfolio was fantastic.... I like you. Very much."

"But," I said, sighing. I closed my eyes momentarily, dreading the next thing he would say. And yet, there was the business of the kiss that seemed confusing now. I lowered my chin, studying my now empty hands in my lap.

"Yes. There is a but. Don't look like that, Jacqueline. Not until I get this confession out in the open. God help me." He reached a tentative finger beneath my chin and raised it. "That's better," he smiled. "You *are* quite lovely, you know."

"But," I urged, my eyebrows raised, wanting to get it over with.

"Yes. Well. I feel like a teenager saying this...but I spent much of the evening thinking about you in a romantic sense, rather than a business sense — which is terribly unfair to you. Totally unprofessional. Which led me to kiss you rather unexpectedly. And, frankly, now that I've kissed you once, I am finding it extremely difficult to think of anything else except kissing you again...and, well, more, if you catch my meaning... which is quite distracting because of the long

136

drought in my romantic history, not to mention outrageously presumptuous and not at all appropriate —"

I placed one forefinger on his lips. "Stop babbling and kiss me again."

"Are you sure?" Carl whispered. "Because if I kiss you again, Jacqueline, I may never stop...."

The lips that kissed me the following morning were every bit as insistently gentle as they had been the night before. I allowed myself to sink into the pleasure of what those lips could do, then turned the tables, leaving Carl breathless. "You are like a Goddess," he whispered later as we lay side-by-side,. He traced his fingertips across my naked breasts, down the curve of my waist, and over my hips.

"You know, the Goddess insists all acts of love and pleasure are her rituals." I kissed his delectable lips as I ran my fingers down his muscled abdomen.

"Then I am the luckiest man on earth," he smiled, pulling me into his arms.

Carl Jacobs Martin proved to be every bit the unrelenting persistent booger I'd dubbed him Memorial Day weekend. Baring no expense, he traveled to Northern California from his Los Angeles office most weekends, taking me out to one of Sonoma Valley's fine dining establishments, his mind set on enjoying Saturday evening with me and only me, then spending a delightful night beneath my sheets. That magical Sonoma summer I found myself falling in love with the Carl who hid behind the smooth suave facade he wore to face the world, the agent who cared too much about his flighty clients, the man who supported his aging parents without complaint *and* his soon-to-be-ex-wife because she was the mother of his children. Not to mention the father devoted to his daughters despite the inherent difficulty the custody suit posed.

Sundays he visited Hannah and Eloise who lived with their mother in Carl's waterfront Sausalito apartment home. I didn't go with him to see his daughters — he was still embroiled in a contentious legal separation from Victoria — and he wanted not a hint of an excuse to tip the woman sideways and quash the proposed joint custody agreement. Instead, I put my name in the lottery for a spot at the local street markets, and manned my booth when I was lucky enough to be selected.

As usual, my ex, Jim, and his companion, Timothy, helped me with the heavy work. I'd told them about Carl, and Jim had been pleased to hear I was dating. "You deserve to find someone special, Jacks," he said. "Like I found Timothy."

At this declaration Timothy grinned and placed his thin hand on Jim's shoulder, a rare public display for the gay couple, despite living in liberal San Francisco. "When I came out at sixteen, my mom, she told me 'Never say no to love'. I say it to Jim last year, and now we are living together. I say it to you now, Jacks: Never say no to love. Don't let it pass you by."

So I took Jim and Timothy's advice didn't say no when Carl invited me to Los Angeles in September. He and I did, however, have a negotiation on who would pay the airline fare.

"I insist," Carl said on the phone, his voice adopting that adamant persistence I'd grown to expect.

"*I* insist," I countered, not wanting to patently accept him paying for everything. "I can pay my own way."

"I don't know how you afford your apartment and car payment on your salary, never mind groceries. Darling, I make four times what you do, and I am the one inviting *you* to accompany me to this boring fund raising gala. I—"

"Well," I interrupted, "That doesn't mean I can't—"

"I want you with me, Jacqueline," he interrupted back. "I'm tired of going to these events alone. And I'm tired of everyone I know pushing me toward anyone pretty and single. I want the world to see this beautiful love in my life. I don't care whether Victoria finds out. I won't allow her to run my life anymore."

"Are you certain?" I asked the question despite the fact I'd never heard Carl so certain.

"Please bring your gorgeous self to LA. I would be happy to procure your ticket. We can travel back to the Bay Area together Sunday morning. I have a little trip planned for Sunday afternoon, if you're available?"

Hearing the smile in Carl's voice, I became curious. "A trip? Where?"

"Just outside the city. A place I think you'll like. A picnic lunch maybe. Sound good?"

"Sure," I shrugged, thinking no more of it. "Should I bring the amethyst dress, or the black?" I pictured the long black dress with the very low front Carl had admired the last time he was in town.

"The black would be my choice. That way I can spend the evening imagining how I'll have my way with you in the back of the limousine when I free your lovely breasts from that confining fabric."

"Stop," I shushed. "Now I'll be thinking about that throughout the entire event."

"Exactly my plan, Jacqueline."

The gala was classic Hollywood, all the pretty people dressed to the nines turning out to support the newly-formed California Coast Club, whose mission was to man ocean-side cleanup initiatives, including sea animal protection, trash removal, and coastal trail maintenance. Glittering chandeliers lit polished oak floors, while round tables dressed in linen sparkled with cut crystal glasses and silver cutlery. With his smooth and suave persona firmly in place, Carl Jacobs Martin introduced me to his business contacts and partners and clients and friends — too many to count — garnering more than a few catty looks from a number of shapely beautiful women.

The dinner menu was farm-raised salmon covered in fresh pesto, with summer vegetables on a bed of jasmine rice. Wine flowed freely, as did the guest's checks, to help fund the Coast League startup costs. It was a good cause and most wealthy Californians love nothing more than helping protect the natural environment.

Dressed in a tailored tuxedo with tails, Carl was in his element, one of the most handsome and gregarious men in the room. He swept me out onto the dance floor for a quick waltz as the evening waned, his cheek nuzzled against my temple. "Are you ready to shed that lovely dress yet?" he teased, his warm hands touching the bare skin on my back.

"Are you ready to coax it off me?" I smiled, eyebrows raised.

"I don't need to be invited twice." He took me by the hand and propelled me quickly toward the door.

In the privacy of the limousine, Carl turned his undivided attention to fulfilling his promise. The ride back to his LA condominium went exactly as planned, the dress unceremoniously finding its way onto the floor. Not that some of Carl's clothing wasn't soon cast aside as well, although by the time the driver opened the door to usher us out, we were once again decently clad, if not a bit ruffled. Until safely ensconced in the foyer behind closed doors, where Carl's soft lips persuaded me to immediately disrobe again.

Chapter Five

Sunday morning I awoke to the smell of breakfast. Scrambled eggs and toast, with orange juice and coffee, delivered by my smiling lover. The polished wood breakfast tray held a single red rose, the scent a sweet accompaniment to citrus and strong coffee.

"I love seeing you here in my bed," Carl laughed. "Say you'll stay for a while?"

"You know I love you, but you know I can't," I mumbled, my mouth full of eggs.

"I understand." Carl opened the closet and chose some casual khakis and a dark green Henley. "But that doesn't mean I won't stop wishing otherwise."

The flight from LA to San Francisco passed quickly and our Sunday afternoon drive began in pleasant sunshine, the traffic blessedly light. Carl took us south down the Santa Cruz Highway, then up Glen Canyon Road, the black BMW handling the turns easily.

"There's a place up here I think you'll like," he said.

"We passed a lovely park a little ways back, and I thought you'd stop." I pointed behind us.

"This place I'm taking you is actually quite park-like. Big trees, a rose garden. You'll love it."

Turning onto a side-street, we slowed as the road thinned, then pulled down a gravel driveway a few moments later. Tree limbs curved over the drive, creating a tunnel of sorts for about thirty feet, then a Spanish-style ranch came into view. The stucco house held a covered porch along the front, arched columns topped with a red tile roof. Twisted wrought-iron railings linked the columns, the black metal in each section curled into S-shaped designs originating from a central point. The driveway curved along the front of the house in a u-shape, the belly of the u holding an overgrown rose garden.

"Look at the beautiful railings!" I said, captivated by the simple lines. "It's like an image of a weather pattern, great winds swirling."

Carl parked the car and smiled. "Care to take a look around?"

"This is someone's home, not a park." I breathed in a pleasant whiff of rose streaming through the car window.

"One of my clients asked me to take a look at it. He's thinking of buying it. I have a key." He

144

dangled a set of keys in his hand. "I'd like your opinion. Then we can look for a picnic spot."

"Sure," I shrugged. "I'd love to see the inside. Is it empty?" I exited the car to follow him, thankful I'd brought tennis shoes to wear with my faded jeans.

"Yes," Carl said, mounting the terracotta front steps. The front door was crafted from dark wood, the shape artfully arched. "He said the place needed some repairs."

The terracotta tile continued through the foyer and into a sunken great room, the cream-colored walls textured in plaster, some of which was flaking badly to display the lathe beneath. The opposite wall held floor-to-ceiling windows, that looked out on a large terracotta patio with a swimming pool, also in disrepair, the water green and filled with fallen leaves.

"The view out the back is lovely, although the pool is badly in need of care," I offered.

"Yes, I guess the previous owner let the place go somewhat." Carl nodded.

I walked from room-to-room, admiring the bones of the house, while ignoring the peeling paint, broken tile, and bits of crumbling plaster. To the left off the great room, a short hallway led to a large kitchen with chipped tile countertops and a dining area that also featured a window wall. On the opposite side of the house, the master bedroom offered arched patio doors with the same backyard view, a small fireplace in one corner. Two smaller bedrooms occupied the street side of the house. A spiral staircase led to two spacious rooms connected by a catwalk above the great room. The top floor was carpeted in a motley shag, the avocado green an ancient relic from the 1970s.

"The house is fabulous," I said to Carl when we converged on the back patio. "It will be a lot of work to refurbish it, but this place could easily be beautiful again. Quite easily." We sat on the risers leading down to the swimming pool.

"I think you should advise your client to buy it for the right price, then he can hire a contractor to implement repairs and a designer to help him decide how and where to modernize. The kitchen and bathrooms obviously. I'd stick with tile, but perhaps go with a lighter color on the countertops, rather than all the dark reds, add some Native American designs in turquoise and black along the backsplash to liven the place up." My thoughts spiraled to different images, bold geometrics and rustic wood accents.

"The place is almost like a blank canvas," Carl mused. "Someone could do anything they wanted. Wouldn't you say?"

"Yes," I gazed up at the towering bay trees. "Mosaic would blend nicely with this architecture, or murals, if they found the right painter. Leather, or even rattan, furniture would go well with the terracotta, you know an outdoor living motif with such a wonderful span of windows." I turned to wave at the house at our backs.

"What about the upstairs?" Carl asked the question casually, his expression thoughtful.

"Those rooms need skylights," I said immediately, "to lighten them up. Not to mention new flooring. Definitely a bathroom upstairs too. It could go directly above the one adjacent to the foyer, easier to plumb the water wall that way. I'd put in an outdoor shower here somewhere too. Why not? The property is private and it would be a nice way to rinse off after swimming."

"You'd keep the pool, then?"

"Definitely." I studied the murky green water. "But he might want to add a hot tub. There." I pointed to the side by the master bedroom.

"Yes. That's a great idea."

"So you think he'll buy it?" I didn't ask who the client was; Carl rarely used names and I respected the way he protected his charge's privacy.

"He is actually buying it for his lady love," Carl smiled. "He wanted it to be an engagement gift when he asked her to marry him."

"That's wonderful. I'm sure she'll love it... provided they know how much work it is going to be. These repairs could be quite extensive. Not to mention expensive. They probably couldn't move in for a while."

"He's quite clear about that. But he thought she'd love the place and embrace it as a project. She's an artist, you see."

"I can definitely appreciate how an artist would love this place." I took a deep breath and moved my legs to the side to stand. "So, are you ready to find a spot to open a picnic basket?"

"In a minute," Carl said, placing his hand gently on my arm. "I have one more question for you."

I gazed up at his handsome face. He seemed suddenly troubled, uncomfortable, unsure. "Okay." Curious, I waited for him to formulate the words.

"I want to do this right," he said, kneeling beside me on the dusty riser. He took my hand in his, the warmth radiating through me the way it always did.

I looked into his gray eyes, a murky sea color today paired with the forest green shirt. His uncertainty was somewhat out of character and I felt at once perplexed and concerned, until he spoke again.

"Jacqueline, I realize everything has happened quickly between us, but..." Drawing a small box out of his shirt pocket, he opened it to reveal an emerald ring, surrounded by small glittering diamonds. "I love you like no other. Will you marry me?"

Stunned, I looked from the ring to the sincere man and back again. To say the proposal was unexpected would be the understatement of the year. I absolutely hadn't seen this coming. Words clogged in my mind as tears welled in my eyes.

Carl cleared his throat, "it would be nice if you said *something*, even if that something is 'hell no.'"

"I'm sorry," I rasped, lurching sideways into his arms. "I'm just so flabbergasted, I don't know what to say."

"I'd hoped you would say yes," Carl spoke the words into my neck as he held me tight.

"Yes," I managed, still tearful. "But..." I pulled back to wipe my eyes, "you aren't divorced, are you?"

"No," Carl admitted. "But I instructed my lawyer to ditch the separation documents and we filed the initial divorce paperwork earlier this week. So I will be. Hopefully quite soon. And I wanted to tell you... to show you... how I am so completely in love with you. I want to spend every day with you. Every night. I never want us to part. I've convinced the agency to open a San Jose office, so I can move up here permanently." Carl paused and looked away, then stood and drew me to my feet. He turned me by the shoulders to face the stucco house. "This house is mine, Jacqueline. I bought it last week.

"For you.... Well, for us. Please say yes."

Chapter Six

The decision to move in with Carl proved to be an easy one, made all the more easy by my Santa Rosa employer offering me remote contract work without batting an eye, ensuring I did not have to commute — or resign. The most immediate complication was my apartment lease. I didn't want to bag out on it and end up with any legal mess. Although Carl offered to pay it off and be done with the commitment, I felt uncomfortable with him simply taking care of it for me. I did not want to be one of the people in his life who depended on him financially. I wanted to pay my own way — at least at the level I could pay — while also respecting the salary differences between us and allowing him to bear the brunt of an expense because he could.

The weekend I packed my things, I called my cousin Rita. Her wedding was in a month and I needed to make travel arrangements. Besides, we needed to plan a bachelorette party. I was thinking we'd all go to a club, maybe one of those male stripper places. Rita would definitely be up for that, as would most of our New York girlfriends. Rita's phone rang and rang, until she finally picked up. I could tell something was amiss the moment she slurred hello.

"Rita? Why are you drunk already on a Sunday?" Morning drinking was a bad, bad sign in my book, a world-is-surely-ending sign.

"Gabriel fucking Capellani boned that slut Maria Espinoza — remember her from sixth grade? — then fell hopelessly in love with the bitch. And now...." Rita's voice fell silent and I could tell she was swallowing her tears.

"Now what?" I prompted, guessing Rita had probably kicked the bastard out.

Sniffing loudly my cousin continued. "Now he's broken our engagement off and shitfire, Jacks, it hurts like a motherfucker." Rita broke down in sobs, something I'd never heard despite knowing the woman my entire life.

Three thousand miles away, all I could do was listen. My cousin was like a sister to me. We'd gone to school together and spent every summer together for as long as I could remember. Her mother and mine had been close sisters and we'd lived in the same neighborhood and attended the same schools our entire childhood.

"Fucker," I muttered, thinking Gabriel Capellani deserved to have his ball sack kicked up his rectum. Maybe I could get my brother Ernie to track him down and do the dirty deed.

"Damn right." Rita flicked her lighter, then took a drag off her cigarette.

"Did you tell your mom?" I cringed as I asked the question, suspecting Rita hadn't — because if she had I would certainly have heard the news by now. The woman would go ballistic when she found out her daughter had been practically left at the altar.

"Nope."

"Are you kicking him out?"

"Didn't have to. He left. Moved in with Maria as a matter of fact." Rita firmed her voice. "I can't stay here in this apartment, Jackie. I just don't have it in me." The tears came again, softer this time. "I just wish I knew why...you know, why I had to fall in love with the wrong guy...."

I listened to my cousin cry, feeling angry and protective. She'd fallen hard for Gabe and I knew the betrayal was ripping her lungs out. This wasn't something Rita would bounce back from easily as she had her other boyfriends.

"Sometimes there is no explanation, honey. We love who we love." Helplessly I wracked my brain for something comforting to say, a part of me knowing nothing would take the deep hurt away. But getting Rita away from town for a while might help her gain some perspective.

"Just fucking leave," I blurted. "Get out of New York. A change of scenery might—"

"And go where, Jacks? I don't have the energy for it." The characteristic fizzing of a beer bottle popping open accompanied the flat statement.

"Come to Santa Rosa."

"And live with you? Yeah, sure. I'd drive you crazy and you know it."

Rita was right. We'd tried living together one summer as teenagers at our grandparents cottage on Cape Cod. She was the messiest housekeeper I knew. Her disorder made me want to scream. But I wouldn't be in Santa Rosa long.

"I'm moving to Santa Cruz with Carl," I said, keeping my voice casual. "You'd be doing me a favor if you'd consider subleasing my apartment. Until you figure out what you're doing. I could leave it fully furnished. All you'd have to do is bring yourself and a suitcase or two."

"Yeah?"

I let the idea percolate, giving my cousin time to think. Pushing Rita to do anything always backfired. I had to let her get used to the idea first, then deliver the deciding blow.

"I dunno, Jackie...."

"What else you gonna do with all that wedding cash you saved up working at Filene's? Might as well take some time off and figure out some things, right? Fuck Gabe. You ain't gonna moon around Queens with everyone whispering behind your back. Just leave it all behind in your rearview mirror. You got better things to do."

"Fucking right I got better things to do," Rita rasped. "Fuck Gabe. Fuck Maria. Fuck the whole damn nosy neighborhood. Maybe I *should* just up and leave." The last sentence sounded determined, more like the Rita I knew.

"Do it, Rita. Just... do it. You'll be glad you did. Call me when you book your flight," I said, pushing the idea a bit now that it sounded like my cousin might actually take my advice. "I'll pick you up at the airport. You don't have to stay forever. Just for a while. Until you're ready to go back." Of course, there was always the possibility that, like me, Rita might never go back. But that was a subject for another conversation.

"I'll call the airline today, Jacks. I promise I will. And...you know, thanks." With that my cousin hung up the phone, hopefully to bite the bullet and tell everyone the wedding was cancelled. No one in our family would be happy to hear she was leaving — they hadn't been too keen when I left five years ago with Jim either — but sometimes getting away from an old life was the only way to create a new one.

Rita arrived a week later with three oversize suitcases in tow — I guess she thought she might stay a while. After playing tour guide and showing my cousin the San Francisco Bay Area for a week, I departed, leaving the apartment in her care. I hoped she'd embrace a new start, but it wasn't something I could do for her.

154

Chapter Seven

I refurbished the Glen Canyon house as Carl and I planned, embracing the project as a blank canvas. The empty walls became life-size murals, depicting flowering garden scenes, with stone doorways slightly ajar showing a slice of a mystical mythical world beyond. Unbeknownst to me, Carl photographed my work and placed it in his San Jose office suite, where the pieces gained substantial interest. So I became a mural painter for the Silicon Valley nouveau rich, while working alongside Carl every so often as a graphic artist to help his clients' side-businesses.

My transition to Santa Cruz was easier than I dared imagine. I made friends with some of the musicians and artists in the area, folks who appreciated my differentness and didn't expect me to present a posh and polished exterior. Rita visited every other month without fail, lounging by my refurbished pool and helping me paint walls or pick out bathroom fixtures or weed the rose garden — willing to do whatever was needed and bringing her characteristic caustic charm. Jim and Timothy passed through occasionally when Jim was playing in Santa Cruz, an opportunity for them to leave behind the bustling crowds of the city music scene and enjoy the peace and beauty of the canyon.

My relationship with Carl unfolded into a harmonious life filled with remarkable ease, our disagreements few and far between, mostly borne out of creative differences at work when our opinions clashed — although rarely for long. Carl's daughters visited every few months despite their mother's best attempts to block the established visitation arrangement. The girls loved the upstairs bedroom I'd designed for them with rainbow-colored fairies and bright flowers and pony-sized dragonflies on the walls. Victoria's law firm dragged the divorce agreement out, countering every proposal, demanding more money, and finally insisting on custody hearings presided over by a judge, rather than an arbitrator. Eventually, since the parties absolutely could not agree, the matter was finally forced onto a court docket to determine alimony and child support payments.

Long story short: now that I was in the picture, Victoria wanted a boatload of cash and Carl had reached the end of his patience. And his savings.

He and I couldn't marry until his divorce was finalized of course, and although I felt I was already married to the man in many ways, Carl desperately wanted things settled. The frustration with Victoria's lawyers and the ridiculous delays had him at his wit's end. No matter how often I assured him I was with him for the long haul and that we simply needed to wait it out, he still got quite upset over it periodically. He wanted us to be married, for our relationship to be official. Recognized. Legal. I did too, but nothing he'd tried could get Victoria to budge. So we simply waited.

Almost a year later on Christmas Eve, we decided to go to brunch to celebrate the holiday season and discuss the most recent legal developments. I'd been feeling a bit off, tired and achy as if a cold was brewing, but Carl very much wanted to do something special, so I dressed and we headed to the Santa Cruz waterfront.

Our favorite restaurant boasted ocean views from every table. Although busy, the wait staff knew us and treated us like royalty.

"So, what adventure should we go on tomorrow? Fisherman's Wharf? Maybe the beach?" Smiling, I attempted to weave some holiday cheer into a conversation I knew might become frustrating when he caught me up on the details of Victoria's latest demands.

Shifting uncomfortably in his seat, Carl avoided my eyes. "There's been a lot of pressure for me to spend Christmas with the girls this year. My lawyer said there was a good chance that if I didn't, Victoria would use that as the final bit of leverage to prove I was an uninterested parent and therefore undeserving of any joint custody arrangement."

"That's ridiculous! The girls are in Vail with your parents taking ski lessons every day and having the time of their lives. On your dime! You're flying out to collect them over the weekend, right? Are you thinking you should go a few days sooner?"

"I — I do, actually." Carl placed his warm hand atop mine, his thumb rubbing my emerald engagement ring. "Except...well...I'm thinking I should go this afternoon. You know, surprise them Christmas Eve."

"I see," I said, the picture becoming clear. "But I'm not invited, am I?" The question was rhetorical and we both knew it. Carl was choosing his family over me — they were, of course, his darling daughters. But on Christmas Eve on a moment's notice, leaving me alone for the holiday? That really took the proverbial cake. Carl was speaking again, offering yet another apology and justification, the same old story I'd heard a thousand times.

"I'm sorry Jacks...you'll of course join us next year after the divorce is final. With the settlement so close, I just don't want to upset the applecart."

"Of course." My voice became sarcastic. "Victoria is *still* running your life. No, actually, she's running *our* life. I'm tired of this, Carl — this game where you and I are jerked all over the place because of her demands."

I was actually beyond tired. I was absolutely sick of it. Carl's decision to placate her expectations and abandon me on Christmas hit me in a place that stung like crazy. I could barely contain my anger. I wanted to scream at him and rant. But I didn't. Because we were in a public place. Which is exactly how Carl planned it. Chicken-shit ass-hat.

Determined to end the discussion and our brunch, I stood and calmly said my piece. "In fact, I'm not only tired of the game, I'm forfeiting the match." Then I walked from the restaurant, seething.

Outside, I nodded for the valet to fetch the car. Carl appeared at my side, as I suspected he would.

"Jacqueline," he murmured, "Please. I—" He placed his hand lightly on my forearm.

"Don't," I warned, my voice an angry growl. "Just don't...."

The valet pulled the BMW to the curb and I stepped forward, my palm against Carl's chest. "Call a cab to take you to the airport," I instructed, my serious eyes meeting his. "We'll talk about things when you return. I'm not going to do anything rash...I just need some space." Then I squared my shoulders and walked away. When I stomped on the gas, the BMW responded quickly, tires squealing in protest.

I didn't look back until it was almost too late to see Carl wave goodbye.

Chapter Eight

My old apartment looked much the same as I'd left it. Rita had kept my furniture, but decorated the walls with the artwork she preferred: mostly ocean scenes, seals and dolphins, colorful underwater landscapes. I turned on the Tiffany stained glass lamp in the living room and stowed my luggage beneath the kitchen table. Given the fact it was Christmas Eve, my cousin was out, probably enjoying the evening with her new beau. No matter. She wouldn't care if I made myself at home.

Knowing Carl would head back to the house to pack before leaving, I drove immediately to San Jose and stopped at a mall to augment my wardrobe. The new wheeled leather luggage cost me an arm and a leg, but I figured that's what credit cards were for. I placed the case of Heineken I'd purchased in Rita's refrigerator, where I tore open a corner and extricated a pleasantly cold green bottle.

Merry fucking Christmas, I thought, popping the top and taking a gulp.

Beer in hand, I headed toward the living room couch, when the door suddenly flew open and crashed against the wall. The sound frightened me out of my wits, but that was the least of my worries. Into the room jumped a woman in a black leather coat, fishnet stockings and high heels, screaming like a banshee. The banshee's face was twisted into a fierce grin, teeth bared as she howled like a madwoman, her hands curled into fists.

I threw the beer bottle in her direction and leaped for the couch where my purse sat holding the only weapon I could think of on short notice — a bottle of pepper spray. Fortunately the banshee came to her senses before I could extricate the weapon and use it.

"Jackie?" the woman said, staring at me.

"God damn it, Rita. You scared the crap out of me." Indignant, I stomped into the kitchen to grab a towel to sop up the beer spill.

"What the hell are you doing here?" She stumbled to a kitchen chair and leaned her head in her hands on the glass tabletop as if to hold it on her neck.

"I could ask you the same thing." I studied the crinkled bow on my cousin's head and the fishnet stockings. "Looks like you were on your way to one hot party. What happened? You look a mess, girlfriend."

"Look who's talking," Rita said, nodding at my wrinkled silk dress. "You drive up this afternoon?"

"Damn right I did," I bristled. "Son of a bitch springs the news on me at brunch today. No big deal. He's flying out to spend Christmas with his daughters in Vail. Skiing. *'Sorry Jacks...of course you'll join us next year after my divorce is final...'* Fucking asshole." I retrieved two fresh beers from the refrigerator and motioned toward the sofa. "Care to join me getting shitfaced drunk?"

"Don't mind if I do," Rita said, stripping the hairclip and rumpled golden bow off her head. "Meet you on the couch after I put on something decent." She kicked off her black high heels, one skittering across the kitchen linoleum.

"Who was he, Reets?" I asked, understanding that something had gone quite wrong for Rita to be home on Christmas Eve.

"Nobody important," she scoffed, and turned away. "Not anymore."

The following morning I emerged from the shower to hear Rita yell goodbye and slam the phone receiver down to convince herself she meant it.

"I guess you told him," I said, leaning against the hallway doorframe with a towel wrapped around my torso.

"Yup. My turn to hit the shower. Coffee's in the cabinet above the stove."

An hour later the two of us sat sipping our second cup of coffee together in the living room. Despite the fact we looked like a million bucks, beneath the veneer we were both heartbroken, ready to cry at a moment's notice.

"So, what are you going to do, Jacks?"

Rita's question jogged me out of my pathetic reverie. What was I going to do? A delicious thought bloomed in my brain. "I think I am booking a ticket to Vail, Colorado to take ski lessons from one of those handsome former Olympians."

"Brilliant." Rita smiled. "And I wonder who you might see there?"

"Don't matter," I shrugged, smiling to myself. "You think with all the partying Christmas crowd I'm going to be spending too much time all by my lonesome? My friend Virginia offered me a bunk in her condo, and she and her fiancé aren't staying more than a few days, so I'll have the place to myself and whoever I decide to play with."

"You are an evil woman, Jackie." Rita nodded her approval, painted eyebrows raised.

"Let's see what the cards say about that, shall we?" I jumped to my feet and headed toward the spare room, my new red rayon pantsuit rustling. "I'll have to do something about this stuff you're storing for me one of these days, Reets. Do you mind if it stays for now?"

"I don't use that room, so it's fine to leave it. But my lease expires in July, so we should talk before then in case I decide to move."

"Here they are." I returned to the living room and opened the colorful box.

"Tarot?" Rita asked, curious.

"Yeah. I stumbled on it when Jim and I first moved out to California. Everyone seemed very into getting readings at the time. Maybe it *was* just a fad, but I found I really liked it. Like the cards spoke to me in some way. An old neighbor gave me her deck when she moved." I shuffled the cards, stilling my mind and silently speaking the prayer I always said when preparing for a reading: *May the unknown become known. May I be a clear messenger. May I be in service to the divine.*

"So how do you do a reading then?" Rita leaned forward with interest.

"There's a lot to Tarot. I could go on about the history and symbology, but some of it is really quite simple. Me, I run with the first feeling or image I see in the card, allowing the reading to unfold as it will. Today I'll do a short four-card reading to answer a specific question I have in mind. In this case, whether to go to Vail."

Cutting the cards into three piles, I assembled the deck in a different order, then placed four cards face down: the past, present, challenge, and outcome cards, each to be read in order left to right.

The first card I turned was the King of Wands wearing a fiery red cloak. My past as it related to my current question. A vivacious and energetic King, a passionate man, a magnanimous father. Definitely the Carl I knew and had fallen in love with three years ago.

The present situation was depicted by the Four of Wands, a man and woman dancing together in a pavilion. Romance, an engagement, a celebration of home. Such a beautiful representation of our Glen Canyon life.

The challenge card was the Page of Cups, a young lady standing by the seashore holding a glowing cup out of which a fish stood on its tail. Tapping the card with one chipped fingernail, I paused, thoughtful. "This card almost always means good news. Sometimes a pregnancy." I shook my head at that thought, and continued. "But today this card reminds me of Carl's daughters. They are actually wonderful kids most of the time, but quite energetic and demanding of his attention. When they visit, I hear a perpetual chorus of "Daddy look at me." Both he and I end up exhausted by the girls' unceasing intensity. I know it's just kids being kids, but they are *definitely* a challenge. And they do present the complication in this situation for sure."

I turned the outcome card, the Nine of Wands reversed, a man standing behind a fence of wands, leaning on a staff. "This is the dig in and wait and see card," I said. "Delays and obstacles. Adversity.

Sometimes, with the reverse interpretation, a dead end. I know this sounds terrible, but it's really been the story of my life with Carl. We've been waiting for the lawyers to settle things with the divorce and it is just taking so damn long, we get frustrated. This card tells me the outcome is still stalled. Nothing is going to change. In fact, things may be delayed further. No surprise there. It is what it is. Might as well accept it and move on."

Sighing, I gathered the images, reviewing them one more time. "So when I think about the question of whether I should go to Vail, this outcome points to the possibility of travel delays, and more frustration on top of the current frustration. As lovely as a skiing trip sounded earlier, I don't know whether that's what I should be doing. Going home and enjoying the peace and quiet, or perhaps catching up on my design work for Carl's new executive placement agency feels like a better use of my time. He'll be delighted to come home to a new set of logos and letterhead designs to jump start his creative process."

I shrugged, disappointed but resolved, and smiled. "Now that that question is settled, let's read you." I looked over at my cousin. "Think about your question while I shuffle."

"I don't know, Jacks." Rita shifted uncomfortably on the couch. "I essentially just told Dave to take a flying leap. I don't know there's anything to read."

Considering what to say to my cousin, I nodded. "Last night you mentioned that blonde, Candy, had been an old girlfriend, but he'd been the one to break it off, right? I know you saw what you saw... but what if there's something else you need to know. A bigger picture. This is actually one of my favorite types of readings. In this case, the question would be something like... 'what do I most need to know about this relationship thing with Dave?' Wanna give it a try?"

I continued shuffling, giving Rita time to come around to my way of thinking. She wanted — no, she *needed* — to understand what had happened with Dave. And what might happen in the future. I hoped the cards would have an answer for her.

"Ready?" I asked, laying out four cards in a row.

Taking a deep breath, she nodded. "Ready."

I turned the first card, the Five of Swords, a man laughing as he walks away from a fight with two other swordsmen. "Shitfire, girlfriend, no messing around here. I call this card the humiliation card. In this case, a past defeat that involved some shady underhanded tactics. A failure where nobody wins. This card is the past, but I don't know whether it is yours or his. Maybe both."

The second card, the present, was the Magician, a mystical man with the tools of his alchemical trade displayed on a table before him. "This card represents intention. Imagination. Will combined with skill. Competence and confidence. Again, whether we're reading him or you Reets, this is a very strong card. Let's see if the other cards make things any clearer."

Turning the Seven of Pentacles, I frowned, trying to piece together the relationships between the images to tell the story. The card showed a youngish man in a garden surrounded by golden pentacle blossoms, the fruit of his labor.

"Wealth is the challenge?" Rita asked.

"It's more than that," I said. "It is waiting for investments to mature, or your work to bear fruit, which requires time and a lot of patience. I think patience is the challenge here. Sometimes the wine has to mature to develop that rich taste we so love. Make sense?"

"I think this reading is about Dave *and me*," Rita said, "as if we're on parallel paths in some way."

"Could be," I said, turning the outcome card.

Both of us stared at the unpleasant image of two paupers in the snow outside a lovely stained glass church window. The window contained five pentacles gleaming in warm red and green and gold hues. This was one of my least favorite cards in the deck, but I read it anyway. "This is the 'left out in the cold' card. It can pertain to financial failure, or loss of a lover. Often it signifies homelessness — either literal or figurative. Once I saw this card interpreted as the catch 22 of a Catholic marriage, where fealty comes at all costs

— including your own personal happiness. But beyond that, it's alienation, feeling cast out. Alone." I looked over at my cousin. "I'm having trouble putting this reading together, Reets. What do you think?"

Clearing her throat, Rita wiped her eyes on a battered napkin she'd stuffed into the cuff of her orchid cashmere sweater. "You do realize this card is pretty damn close to where I stood last night looking in the window of Dave's cabin at his Christmas lights?"

"Oh God, Reets. I didn't think. I'm so sorry." Inwardly cringing, I reached across the couch to touch my cousin's hand.

"No. Don't be." Rita shook her head, tapping the first card, the Five of Swords. "The humiliation card...I definitely relate to that. Been there, done that. In spades. And apparently I haven't progressed a whole lot because I'm doing it again with this alienation card. Fuck."

Shaking her head, Rita studied the image of the Magician, as if trying to put together the meanings. "But this Magician and the patience card sound like a different story, don't they?"

"Could be, but it usually doesn't work that way. I think this is a story about *someone*," my voice emphasized the word someone so Rita knew it was perhaps not only her, "who had a messy humiliating love affair in the past, but is coming into his or her own, as represented by the Magician. That someone is experiencing the

170

challenge of waiting until the time is right to grab the success — or the love — they've waited for and worked hard to manifest. The current outcome... I think this means if they fail the challenge... could very likely make them feel alone, left out in the cold. An island so to speak." I paused, considering the card meanings, then continued. "The question we asked for this reading was 'what do I most need to know about this relationship thing with Dave,' right? I'm guessing the cards are telling you more about your dynamic, but as you said earlier, your lives may be running in parallel and the story is both of yours. The thing to remember — and this is important, Reets — the outcome is reading the current trajectory of events. All that can change if we somehow decide to make different choices."

A pounding knock on the door startled both of us. "Rita, are you there?" a man shouted.

"What the hell?" I gathered up the cards, alarmed.

"It's Dave," Rita said, her hands suddenly shaking. "Oh God. I don't want to see him, Jacks. I didn't think he'd come here. Shit. What am I gonna say?"

"You're gonna go in the bedroom and let me handle it," I said, shoving her gently in the back. I swished my hand at her. "Go."

As Rita closed the bedroom door, I unlocked the deadbolt. I was pissed off at the world. Correction: at the men in the world. This Dave

Higgins had ripped my cousin's heart out. Not okay. I wanted nothing more than to rip him back.

"Rita, what the hell... Oh, sorry ma'am, you're not Rita. I must have the wrong apartment."

"No. Right apartment. I'm Rita's cousin, Jackie. And you are...?" I kept my voice cool and detached. I wasn't someone he could mess with and I wanted him to know it.

"Dave Higgins. I'm um... Rita's friend. Maybe she's told you about me?"

I sniffed a laugh. "Yeah. I know the name, Mr. Higgins. I also know a two-faced cheat when I see one. You're not welcome here. So I advise you to get the fuck off my porch before I call the cops."

"Whoa. Just a second there. I don't know what you're talking about ma'am, but you apparently have me mixed up with someone else." Dave sounded taken aback, shocked.

"No I don't think so," I laughed, the sound as derisive as I could make it. "After your little interlude last night with your old lover, a Miss Candycane, Rita doesn't care to see you anymore. I think she told you that already? So please, pursue your affections with this other woman and leave my cousin alone."

"What the hell did Candy tell her?" Dave sputtered.

"Nothin' you need to be concerned about, Mr. Higgins. Now, please leave. I'm asking you nicely."

"Nothing happened, Rita. I swear it. Whatever she told you was a lie." Dave raised his voice so the entire apartment complex could hear him. "Please, honey. Let me explain."

"Don't give me a reason to call the law, Mr. Higgins. I have the phone in my hand."

"God damn it, Rita. Talk to me." Dave shouted, his expression surprisingly desperate.

I dialed the phone, three beeps, then spoke. "Yes, I'm calling to report an attempted break-in at 1243 Sunshine Avenue...."

"All right. I'll go. I don't want any trouble." Dave announced. "But this ain't over, Rita. Not by a long shot."

At the sound of screeching tires I shut the front door and slide the deadbolt into place. "I don't think he'll be back, Reets," I said, returning the phone to the charging cradle. The fake 911 call had accomplished what I intended.

Opening the bedroom door, Rita stumbled into my open arms. "Jacks, I'm just so...." My cousin's voice cracked, the strain too much. "I can't believe this is happening to me again," she sobbed. The tears came in a debilitating flood. I enfolded her into a hug and we both collapsed onto the carpet, our backs against the wall.

We love who we love, and the pain of that loss can be inconsolable.

All I could do was hold her and tell her everything would be all right. Not that she believed me. Because we both knew the heartbreak gig. Time supposedly heals all — or at a minimum takes away some of the hurt. But with Rita I wasn't sure that was true. I'd hoped it was when she left New York to come to California. That she'd eventually get over Gabe, start a new life, and find someone else. But this Dave setback was more devastating than I'd first imagined. I hoped she'd bounce back, but in that moment, I suspected it would take quite a bit longer than either one of us wanted to admit.

Chapter Nine

Christmas night I headed home late after tucking my cousin into bed with a cup of chamomile tea and a good book. I slept most of the next morning away, awakening only when my stomach insisted it needed food. Eating turned out to be a mistake though, because I vomited almost immediately after swallowing the last bite of toast. Chalking the incident up to stress and a late night, I took some fizzy stomach medicine and crawled back into bed, finally rising again at sundown. The feeling of bloated nausea in my stomach persisted, and the achiness I'd felt the past few days had settled in — of all places — my breasts.

I drove to the store in the rain to grab some ibuprofen, my pain reliever of choice. The twisty canyon road turned my mind to the events of the past few days: the incident with Carl in the restaurant, Rita's banshee face as she sprang through the apartment door, the desperation in

Dave's eyes when I insisted he leave my cousin's apartment. The memories collided with tarot card images, a handsome Carl smiling as the King of Wands, a morose Rita standing in the snow outside a brilliant Five of Pentacles stained glass window, Dave watching his garden grow in the Seven of Pentacles.

The final image was me, holding a fish in a goblet as the Page of Cups. I guess sometimes it takes a while for us to understand what the universe is screaming at us.

Once I parked in the grocery store parking lot, I wiped the tears off my face. Then I pulled myself together, bought the ibuprofen I'd come to purchase along with a home pregnancy test, drove home quickly, and peed on the stick.

Later that night I sat in bed with my sketch pad, considering images for Carl's new executive placement agency. I was thinking nouveau tech, colorful and sharp, but also something that invoked old California. Stability and history. I wanted to get a few ideas on paper before Carl returned the following week to prompt his creative mind. I drew columns and arches, climbing grape vines, stylized Mexican flowers, but nothing seemed quite right yet.

The jiggling sound of a key in the front door interrupted my process, my heart throbbing in my chest as I realized someone unexpected was attempting to enter my home. I set the sketch pad aside, and padded out to the great room, the phone in my hand. The jiggling persisted, a muttered curse whispered on the other side of the front door.

"Who's there?" I yelled, using volume to keep the quiver out of my voice. "Be warned, I'm calling the cops right now."

"Please don't, darling," a man's voice said. "I simply can't see well enough to find the lock."

"Carl?" I peered through the peep hole out into the darkness. His return flight wasn't supposed to be until New Year's Eve.

"Is there someone else who calls you darling?"

My lover's exasperated voice made me smile. I opened the door to find a somewhat rumpled and exhausted man, clutching a camouflage day pack.

"I didn't expect you... What's that?" I pointed to the back pack.

"It's all they had at the sporting goods store and I needed something on short notice," Carl shrugged, dropping the bag at his feet. He stepped forward, his hands tentatively gripping my elbows. "I'm so sorry. I should never have left." His gray eyes searched my face, the deep worry evident.

"I should never have walked out of the restaurant." I said, stepping into his embrace and kissing his cheek. "I was so angry — not that I didn't have reason to be — but —"

"You had every right to be. I was capitulating. Allowing Victoria's ridiculous demands to determine my choices. It won't happen again. Ever. I promise." He kissed my forehead and eyelids, then found my lips.

"You came home early," I said a moment later. "What about the girls?"

"I left them with their doting grandparents. Having the time of their lives, as you knew they would," Carl smiled. "I wanted to be here with you."

"Well.... I have something to show you," I said, taking him by the hand. I drew him down the hall to the bedroom.

"This seems promising," Carl chuckled, taking a moment to kick off his shoes.

"It's not that," I admonished, laughing.

As we entered the bedroom, Carl noticed my sketchpads. I released his hand so he could pick one up and study it. "For the new agency?" He nodded his head, thoughtful

"That's not what I wanted to show you."

"No?" Carl turned toward me, his charcoal gray sweater turning his eyes a deep slate.

I handed him the white plastic implement and waited, my face beaming.

"Okay.... ummm. What am I looking at here?" He held the item in his hand, his face perplexed.

"It's positive." I interpreted.

"What exactly does positive mean? I have no idea what this is." Carl flailed the pregnancy test stick in the air.

"I'm pregnant, you ninny." I laughed, aware the bombshell news would undoubtedly be as shocking to him as it had been to me earlier that evening.

"You're what?" Carl's eyes widened as he studied the test results in his hand, the significance of the implement suddenly clear. "Are you sure? Are these things accurate?"

"Well... I have morning sickness and my breasts are swelling like cantaloupes." Suddenly self-conscious, I stood waiting for him to say something. Not that I thought he'd be terribly upset — or at least I hoped he wouldn't be. We'd talked about children, or at least a child. The timing was simply sooner than planned.

Reaching for me again, he gently gathered me into his arms. "I don't know that you could have said anything that would have made me this happy." His voice sounded tearful. "It's the best Christmas gift I could ever ask for. Except for you, of course. And like an idiot I was a thousand miles away..." He sniffed loudly, then wiped his nose on his sleeve.

"Stop," I said, sniffling now too. "We're here together now. All of us."

Carl stepped back and placed his hand on my still flat abdomen. "Yes. All of us. Are you feeling all right, then? Can I get you anything? Perhaps some ginger tea? Ice cream and peanut butter? Hot chocolate maybe?"

"Shut up and kiss me," I laughed.

"Quite gladly," he muttered, his lips against mine. His hands moved up to my waist, then further up my side, then around my shoulders to pause at the spaghetti straps on my top.

"Cantaloupes, you say?" Carl's voice was teasing, his gray eyes shining silver in the muted lighting. "This I must see..." And that was all he said for quite a while.

Chapter Ten

As pregnancies went, mine was rather uneventful. I passed the exhausted nauseous phase quickly and kept to my daily routines, barely missing a beat. Carl suggested I quit my mural work to stay off my feet, but that seemed unnecessary, so I kept painting right into late spring. Until the belly began getting in the way too much and my back ached from leaning forward at the waist to compensate. I put the finishing touches on a pumpkin vine and handed the paintbrush to my new assistant, Josephina.

"Do you think you can you finish it without me?" I asked, my hands massaging my back. The young woman had a talented hand and an eye for color. The design was mine, but the majority of the work would need to fall to her skills on this project.

"Sure. Yes. Don't worry, Ms. Jacqueline. You rest now. This baby is soon, yes?" The young woman's dark brown eyes met mine, then looked shyly away.

"Thank you," I smiled. "I still have a month or so yet. But my step-daughters are coming for a visit tomorrow and I must stop by the grocery store and set up the beds and clean bathrooms, and..."

"I can send my sister Nora to help you."

I smiled at Josephina's offer, an offer she'd repeated ten times in the past month. "No, I can manage," I assured her, feeling protective over my home. Besides, I was fully capable of housekeeping — not that I enjoyed it so very much — but Carl's preliminary divorce settlement had eaten up all of his savings, along with a substantial chunk of his earnings for the present. We weren't exactly struggling, but paying a housemaid was not in my preferred budget. Carl would undoubtedly have a different opinion, but he wasn't there to voice it, so the decision was mine.

On the drive home that afternoon I stopped at the small grocery store at the bottom of the canyon. Carl's daughters had not visited since the previous Thanksgiving. Carl had seen them on his weekend jaunts to Sausalito over the past months, but I hadn't accompanied him. Although the situation with the girls' mother was still awkward — I was called both concubine and harlot on various occasions when Victoria's screeching voice leaked through the phone pressed to Carl's ear — I liked Hannah and Eloise. I wanted to pick up some of the fruit snacks they enjoyed and a few boxes of their favorite cereal to have on hand.

We hadn't yet told the girls I was pregnant. Carl thought it better to do in person while the children were with us so they could get used to the idea without their mother twisting the news into something vile. But the months had slipped by, and now I was quite obviously pregnant, so there would be no hiding it. I hoped the girls would take it in stride and there would be no drama with Victoria when she found out. Because eventually she would. We would not ask the girls to keep a secret from their mother. Unfortunately, if history were any indication, her dramatic responses could and would color the final divorce settlement and custody proceedings.

With his strong feelings about marriage, Carl very much wanted us to be married before our child was born. It was an old-fashioned sentiment that, in the long term, wouldn't matter to anyone except him, but I loved him for wanting to do things right for the daughter in my womb. The ultrasound tech had told us she looked like a she, so for girl's names we picked Jenna and Chloe. We'd know which one was right when we saw her. If the ultrasound tech was wrong, he'd be either a Joseph or a Kirk. Absolutely no Carl Jr.; I didn't want my child to be named after a restaurant chain.

With fruit and milk and cereal in the basket over my arm, I approached the checkout stand. I hadn't bothered to change out of the oversize men's shirt I wore as a painter's smock. With the belly growing, I'd found voluminous clothing more comfortable — especially for work. Our Glen Canyon neighbors knew I was a painter; I didn't need to pretend to be anything else for them. Today I was happily speckled in shades of green with a tad of sapphire sky blue, my hair clipped precariously on the top of my head.

"Hi, James. Beautiful day," I smiled at the long-haired clerk as I hefted my basket onto the counter.

"Hard to be indoors when it's so nice out," the young man agreed, scanning my items with practiced ease. The front door to the grocery chimed open, admitting a blonde woman in sunglasses and two young girls. "Already off work for the day?" James asked.

"Yes," I nodded, "and looking forward to a dip in the pool." I dug my wallet out of my purse.

"Sounds heavenly." The clerk bagged my groceries. "That'll be twenty-eight, fifty seven." Behind me, the mother and daughters arrived at the check stand, the children squabbling over popsicle flavors.

"Orange is the *best*," insisted the smaller child, her hands tugging her mother's purse.

"No way. *Lime* is the best," said the elder, her voice lording her years of expertise over her little sister.

I knew that voice. Turning, I faced the children. "Hello Hannah. Hello Eloise." I smiled, taking great care to sound as casual as possible.

184

"Jacks!" Both girls screamed at once and flew to my side, leaving their well-dressed mother baffled and frowning.

I placed my arms around the children, who found themselves face to face with my pregnant belly.

"What's this?" said Eloise, her hand touching my round abdomen.

"It's a baby," said the older and wiser Hannah. "Or it will be, ninny. We didn't know you were having a baby!"

"Yes, a baby," I confirmed, then met Victoria's eyes. "Jacqueline Carmichael." I politely proffered my hand. "I expected the girls this evening, rather than this afternoon, but no worries."

Victoria stared at my hand as if it were a snake, her mouth in an unattractive frown.

Ignoring the woman's slight, I turned my attention to the girls. "I'm so glad you guys are here. We are going to have such fun this week — "

"Can we do painting?" Eloise interrupted, her small hand tracing the patterns of green on my shirt.

"Can we go swimming?" Hannah jiggled up and down on her toes with excitement.

"Yes, absolutely. We can do both! Your dad —"

"— is a moronic imbecile." Victoria finished my sentence and stared at me. "Go back to the car, girls. I'll be out in a minute."

"But Mom —" Hannah's protest fell on deaf ears.

"Just go, Hannah. Take your sister." The woman's voice rose threateningly and the girl rushed to comply.

"Come on, Eloise," Hannah whispered through clenched teeth, then roughly yanked her younger sister's hand. "We have to go."

Watching the situation unraveling before me, I stuttered a protest. "I could take them up to the house with me now —"

"Not until I've had my say," Victoria hissed, her eyes turning dark. "I can't believe Carl is continuing this ridiculous farce. Subjecting my daughters to such —" she flapped her hand in my direction. "Do you have any idea what you look like?"

Absently I looked down at my work clothes and shrugged. "A painter. I look like a painter."

"You look like a cheap pregnant whore who dug a shirt out of the trash."

"I am not a whore," I growled under my breath. "And I don't appreciate you calling me one at every turn. I suggest you get that through your thick peroxide head."

Victoria laughed at me. The sound cut like a knife. "Oh, but everyone knows you are, dear. All Carl's friends —his partners and colleagues, even his clients." The woman shrugged, her painted lips in a smirk. "Carl Jacobs Martin went slumming and found himself a voluptuous tramp willing to tease and please his precious cock. Many husbands seek the same type of dalliance — those who can afford

186

it anyway. Until they realize how ridiculous they look and return to their wives. He'll leave you sooner than you think. Put it on your calendar. Carl is out of your league, honey. I think you know that already. That bastard you're carrying is probably not even his. I'm willing to bet —"

Dumbstruck by her vehemence and crass assessment, I simply stared at Victoria. Before I could formulate a response, the grocery store clerk's authoritative voice interrupted.

"That's enough, lady." James tossed his stubbly chin to the side. "Get the fuck out of here."

Stunned, Victoria turned to look at the young man behind the cash register. "Are you talking to me?" Her shrill voice began rising. "How dare you speak to me like that?"

"I'll speak to you any way I want," he said, shrugging. "Now, get the fuck out of here."

"I want to see the manager and lodge a complaint," Victoria demanded. "Nobody's check-out boy can be that disrespectful and not expect to get fired."

"I am the manager. Your complaint is noted. Now, for the third time, get the fuck out of my store." The young man pointed toward the door. "And leave the popsicles."

Dropping the frozen juice snacks onto the linoleum floor, Victoria stomped away. I stared at her back as the door closed behind her.

"I'm sorry you had to put up with that, Ms. Carmichael. There's just no excuse for someone to be that rude."

Mutely, I nodded, frustrated tears forming in my eyes. I dared not speak for fear of dissolving into sobs. Did everyone really think that about Carl and me? That I was nothing but a whore. A dalliance, soon to be dumped by the wayside?

"Twenty-eight, fifty seven." The clerk repeated the amount as Victoria drove away.

"Of course," I managed, handing him the cash. "Thank you." I grabbed my three bags and made for the door. I simply wanted to go home and sit by the pool and drink a glass of wine. No, it couldn't be wine. Sparkling cranberry juice, then. And I wanted Carl to tell me that everything Victoria said was vicious lie.

Later that evening, Carl found me in the bedroom, curled into a ball. I'd never made it to the pool. Or the cranberry juice. Instead, I'd crawled into bed and cried myself to sleep, the grocery bags abandoned in the foyer.

"Are you awake, darling?" Carl opened the curtains to let the dusky evening light into the room.

"Yes," I sniffed.

"Victoria called and told me about your grocery store meeting. She'd wanted to drop the girls off early, but instead I put them in a hotel in Santa Cruz. By the ocean."

"Why?" I sat up and blew my nose.

"Because after she told me about your... encounter... I thought it best you and I have the evening alone." Carl sat down on the bed beside me and took my hand.

"Did she tell you what she said to me?" I steeled myself, prepared to get to the bottom of her allegations. If there was any truth to it, I wanted to know. Now.

"Somewhat. I told her she owed my future wife an apology, and that I expected it tomorrow without excuse." Carl firmed his lips. " Seeing you pregnant was apparently quite upsetting. I know she was vile to you, Jacqueline. I think even she would admit it."

I looked over at him, believing his words, but still wanting to know. I didn't want to need reassurance, but apparently I did after Victoria's claims. "Does everyone think I'm a hooker you found slumming and decided to keep? A sexual dalliance you keep around for fun? Someone you'll dump eventually and go back to your wife?" I kept my voice hard, not wanting to believe Victoria, but unable to stop the poisonous thoughts running through my mind. Best to speak them and exorcise them once and for all.

Carl looked in my eyes. "I'm sorry you need to ask me those questions...that she shook your belief in me — in us — so deeply you distrust what we've built here together." He squeezed my hand. "But I'll answer you. And I'll be transparently honest.

"Number one. I found you in a most unlikely place, Jacqueline. At a street fair. Many people know this because they've learned our story. It's no secret. Whether some would call that slumming is up for debate. I don't care and either should you." He held up his free hand to keep my comments at bay, two fingers pointed toward the ceiling. "Number two. As for sex, that's something that is between a couple, yes? But anyone who sees us together can easily see my undisguised and absolute attraction to you. When you are in the room, I cannot look at anyone else. There is no other woman I have ever desired as much as you — I told you this the first night we had dinner together in Sonoma. Whether that constitutes a dalliance, I'd say yes, and it is a most pleasant one. And if others think about us in that light, well then their minds are in the gutter and would be better applied to their own problems. Do I keep you around for fun? Oh, dear God, yes. And last time I checked, I believe the feeling was mutual. But I think you know our relationship is so much more than *that*. You are a remarkable talented woman, and I am the luckiest man on earth to have you in my life." I couldn't help grinning as Carl held three fingers in the air. "As for number three, your final question, it's doubtful I'll grow tired of you anytime soon. If even in this lifetime. In fact, beyond impregnating you with our love child, I have been doing my damnedest to finalize my divorce so I can finally marry you." He leaned toward me and kissed me on the lips.

"You are the love of my life Jacqueline. Please do not let a bitter woman's hurtful words come between us."

Chapter Eleven

"Breathe, Jacks." Rita encouraged me from the driver's seat, her manicured hands placed at two and ten on the wheel. The Glen Canyon turns had tipped my right shoulder against the passenger window where I stayed, eyes closed.

"Slow down," I growled through gritted teeth. My cousin had always driven well above the speed limit and I didn't think today would be any exception — although she perhaps had a valid reason. My back had begun aching that morning and when my water broke, the contractions started. Unsurprising. I was due in a few days. I'd expected the birthing pains to begin slowly, but instead Rita had clocked me at two minutes apart. The doctor's office insisted I get to the hospital ASAP.

"Where is Carl?" I panted between contractions.

"His office said he was out for meetings, so all I've been able to do is leave messages." Rita kept her eyes on the road.

The question of Carl's whereabouts was confusing and frustrating. He knew I was due any day and had wanted to be present at the birth. Assured me he wouldn't miss it for the world. And now he was AWOL? What the hell?

"Jackass," I muttered, "this is all his fault. God damn it, here comes another one." I shifted myself on the seat, suddenly aware that my stomach was threatening to vomit up my breakfast. "Pull over, Rita! Quick. I'm gonna hurl."

Without batting an eye, my cousin stopped in the driveway of a small mansion and handed me a plastic tub from the BMW back seat. "Go right ahead," she said, as if she'd expected it all along.

When we arrived at the hospital, things moved quickly. I was spirited up to the maternity ward in a wheelchair driven by a huge male orderly. I sat very still, panting like a runner trying to stay ahead of the waves of pain, so I didn't scream. Rita followed, my bag on her shoulder, then she helped me undress between contractions. I felt like I had no control over what was happening and I was getting madder by the minute.

"Where is Carl? I asked Rita for the hundredth time.

"I don't know," my cousin said, her eyes troubled, "but it doesn't look like this baby is going to wait for her daddy. "

"Jackass," I muttered again, as the gray-haired maternity nurse checked my progress, her fingers probing inside me.

"We all say something like that at this point, honey. You're almost at seven. The head is down. This baby is well on the way."

Women began moving equipment on rollers into the room. My doctor peeked in and waved, then disappeared before I could ask the man any questions.

As the contractions began to crescendo, I grabbed for Rita's hand at my left. "I can't do this, Reets I'm going to opt for pain medication." Grimacing, I clenched my teeth, steeling myself for the next wave.

"Look at me, Jacks," Rita said, her voice insistent. "Focus. Now relax your body and breathe with me for this next contraction. Then we'll see about medication."

My bulging belly began to contract and my cousin gripped my hand harder. I stared into her eyes and began breathing with her, our whew-whew sounds the only important thing in the room. With my feet in the stirrups and my bare bottom leaking fluid, I tried not to think about anything else except the cadence of my breath.

"Good," Rita said when the contraction passed. "Now chew these ice chips and get ready for the next one."

"I want medication," I insisted.

"Too late for that," Dr. Pollack said, entering the room and rolling a stool to sit by my feet. "You're just about done now, Jackie. Let me check here."

The next contraction came before I could scream at him. Rita began breathing loudly in the Lamaze cadence I'd been taught and I followed her, hanging on to her hand for dear life. If I ever saw Carl Jacobs Martin again, I vowed to slap him.

"Good job. We can see the head now. Almost time to push." The doctor motioned to the nursing staff, who rolled a tray containing a scalpel and sutures beside him.

"What's that?" I asked between breathing sprints.

"It's for just in case it looks like you'll tear. Easier to have a clean cut to repair. OK, now listen carefully. For the next few contractions, you need to push and then stop when I tell you."

"Okay," I agreed, as Rita wiped my forehead with a cool cloth. I closed my eyes to focus. And then we were breathing again and I was pushing and trying not to scream.

At a sudden commotion at the door, I opened my eyes to see my mildly disheveled lover stumble to my side.

"Jacqueline, I —"

"Not now, Carl," Rita interrupted, "she's a bit busy."

I gripped Rita's hand tighter as the contractions rippled through me, the doctor's voice tethering me to consciousness. There was no time to berate Carl, no time to ask questions, no time to do anything except follow the demands of my body and the doctor's instructions. I closed my eyes again to concentrate, reaching blindly with my right hand to find Carl's warm palm. He held my hand, his grip a reservoir of strength I badly needed.

"She's almost here," the doctor said, his encouraging voice suddenly loud in my ears. "One more, Jackie. One more push now."

There was a movement through my torso that felt like it wasn't mine at all. A flexing and a tearing that made me feel like I was being ripped apart. I began crying then, the strain of it all too much, tears flowing uncontrollably down my cheeks, mixing with the sweat.

"It's a girl," Dr. Pollock said.

Then I heard her voice, garbled at first, then louder. My little girl.

Her cry was like a song I'd waited my entire life to hear.

The staff was speaking, moving about with clean linen, rolling a bassinette in through the open door. Carl was patting my hand, his voice a low mumble in my ears. But I didn't hear any of his words. I released the hands at my sides and held my arms out, leaning my torso forward.

"Give her to me," I demanded, my voice cracked and gritty, but strong.

A nurse brought the baby to me, her tiny form wrapped in a white blanket. I settled her in the crook of my arm and laid back on the bed, gazing at the beautiful being who was my daughter. "Hello Jenna." I smiled down at the little girl. "Look at you, baby. Look at you."

"God, she's beautiful, Jacks," sniffed Rita on my left. "Simply gorgeous." My cousin smiled, then blew her nose loudly into a tissue.

"She's made from love," Carl said, his melodic voice quivering. I turned my head to look at him, finding not only Jenna's teary-eyed father, but also a tall black man in a charcoal suit, a bible in his huge hand.

"Where the —"

"I have a lot of explaining to do, but Reverend John here has another event to get to, so if we are going to do this, we have to do it now." Carl's hand cupped my cheek. "If you will..."

"Do what?" I stared at the tall man, my initial impulse to ask the stranger to leave, but then I saw the softness in his eyes as he looked at Jenna.

"Marry you," the reverend said, his deep bass voice filling the room. "If you still want to marry Mr. Martin, that is?" He looked down at Carl, his bushy eyebrow crooked, as if anyone in their right mind would undoubtedly want to think twice about it.

"How..." I couldn't process the events unfolding. I felt Rita's hand on my shoulder, a support and a comfort.

Carl quickly explained, his voice husky with emotion. "We finalized the divorce today. I gave Victoria everything she wanted. Everything. We're broke, Jacqueline, but we're free. John here agreed to come to the hospital and —"

"Aren't you the guy who played running back for that New York team...." my cousin Rita interrupted, staring up at the huge John.

"I was," the big man smiled, "but now folks call me Reverend John. As for this marriage gig, I'm happy to help out my man Carl, but we best get to it, if you don't mind. I'll read the short version, and you both can say your piece." Reverend John chuckled. "Can you be a witness, doc?"

"As soon as I finish stitching this lady up, I'll be glad to give you my John Hancock," Dr. Pollock laughed.

"And you, young lady?" John said to Rita. "Would you be a witness?"

"Hell, yeah," my cousin laughed. "It's about time."

The gray-haired maternity nurse appeared suddenly behind Rita and tucked a small pink rose beside me on the bed. "It was the best I could do for a bouquet on short notice," she smiled, then immediately rushed off.

"All right then." Reverend John cleared his throat, and opened the bible in his large palms. "Do you Jacqueline Carmichael take this man Carl Jacobs Martin...."

I smiled up into Carl's wet eyes, my hands clutching my precious daughter to my chest. "We do, Reverend. By God, we do."

Never Say Goodbye

Sonoma Summers Series (Book 3)

Jesse Devyn Crowe

PHOENIX PUBLICATIONS

ARDENVOIR, WA

*Dedicated to the unexpected road less traveled,
and those we meet along the way...*

Chapter One

Hands cupped together, I flicked the lighter again. The buffeting wind repeatedly snuffed the spark. Finally —about eight tries later — the flame rose long enough for me to draw breath and light the long, thin, cigarette. I took a deep drag, then exhaled slowly, the cool taste of menthol mixing with the smell of salty sea.

Through the murky dark, the sheen of rolling water glistened, the sound of the ocean a wild roar that surrounded me, permeating every cell in my body, as if I were part of the untamed Pacific. The dark silhouette of the cliffs that rimmed the Northern California coast loomed to the south, the beach before me nearly vacant in the pre-dawn light.

Vacant except for me and the harbor seals dozing by the rocks.

Dawn was my favorite time of day. A time when the world changed. When everything became clear. Sometimes that was a wondrous thing, like an angel's wings unfolding. Other times —the mornings after nightmares scoured your mind raw — dawn was the time when things you feared might be true turned out to be all too horribly real. Rarely inconsequential. At least that's how it typically went for me.

This morning was no different. The three hours of sleep I'd managed to snatch had left grit in my eyes and an aching headache. Then again, if I was really being honest with myself, the headache might simply be due to the wine — undoubtedly too much wine. I knew better, but living in the Sonoma Valley, wine was a habit I'd discovered I enjoyed, a ritual I'd adopted to fill the gaping hole in my chest where my heart used to be.

Mostly it worked and I slept it off, oblivious to my own pain. But sometimes, it just made me remember too much. I didn't want to remember, but I did. All too clearly.

The lyrics to an old country song flitted through my mind. Something like "you dun stomped on my heart and you smashed that fucker flat."

"Hear that, Gabe! You asshole!" I cried into the indigo sky. As if anyone was listening. Or cared.

Well, that wasn't exactly fair. Gabe cared. Just not the same way I did. At least not anymore.

"You goddamn selfish asshole..." I whispered, wiping the tears from my eyes and taking another drag from my cigarette.

The light was changing quickly now, the indigo fading to deep lavender, the sky lightening with each passing moment as the earth turned toward the sun and another day began. Another day where I picked myself up, dusted myself off, and tried to stuff my grief back into one of the battered Filene's shoeboxes on my closet shelf.

Most days I managed to sort of forget about Gabriel Capellani, the man who swept me away so completely, and the ivory lace wedding dress I bought to marry him, but never wore. Most days I managed to carry on as if life were my own private magical mystery tour again and the breakup I never saw coming didn't matter at all.

But it mattered. Because I'd never promised anything to any man before Gabe. Before I met that gorgeous Italian, my footloose lifestyle had taken me from one party to another, one boyfriend to another. One hell of a ride from Brooklyn to the Bronx, to college in Albany, then Syracuse, and back again, finally to Queens. No regrets.

But Gabe... Gabe changed everything for me. I fell for him like a bag of rocks tossed off the Queensboro Bridge. He'd fallen for me too — at least that's what he said. Two years later we were engaged and planning a wedding, buying a house, deliriously happy. I was so in love. Until a month before the wedding when he called the whole thing off because he'd become enamored with Maria Espinoza, my best friend from sixth grade, and she with him.

An accident, he assured me. One night playing pool at Rico' Tavern, it just happened — "it" being fucking her in his car instead of simply giving her a ride home, then meeting at her apartment every night after work since. The way Gabe described it, he felt consumed body and soul, a moth to Maria's flame, as if making his infidelity sound poetic would make a difference. "So sorry to have to tell you this Rita after all our plans," he'd said. Because Gabe couldn't marry me when he was so hopelessly in love with *her*.

I didn't believe it at first. How could my fiancé be involved in a romance flourishing right under my nose? I tried to laugh, praying he was pulling my leg. If it was a joke, it wasn't funny. Unfortunately for me, he wasn't kidding. He moved out that same night, while I cried in the bathroom. I hated him for that because I hardly ever cried before Gabriel. He stood there all apologetic and shit, even cried a little himself. Had the gall to tell me I'd always hold a special place in his heart.

Fucker. What the hell was I supposed to do with that? Bottle it and sell it?

I never said goodbye to him. Refused to, actually. I didn't want to think I'd never see him again. Couldn't fathom it at the time. Some days I still couldn't.

To my right, I heard the rustling sounds of the seals slipping into the sea to hunt for breakfast. Or perhaps they were fleeing from the lunatic lady visiting their beach again in the dawn darkness. Flicking the lighter, I checked my watch. Five am. Time to drive back to my Santa Rosa apartment and shower so I could get my ass to work.

Leaving New York had seemed an easy solution to my woes. Run away from the memories Gabe and I made together, the embarrassment of a fiancé cancelling a wedding planned for over a year, the sunny apartment he and I had shared. The choice to come to San Francisco was a trick of fate. A few days after Gabe left, my cousin Jackie rang me up to discuss my bachelorette party. I hadn't had the heart to tell people the wedding was cancelled yet. Jackie listened to my sob story without complaint, on her dime, long distance, then offered me a sublease on her Santa Rosa apartment because she was moving to Santa Cruz with her boyfriend and couldn't get out of the contract.

"Rita, you got better things to do than moon around Queens with everyone whispering behind your back." Jackie'd told me over the phone.

Was my cousin's call coincidence? Maybe. Maybe not.

I preferred the word serendipity. It sounded more sophisticated than fate, less foreign than karma. More akin to something that could happen on the magical mystery tour of life I used to believe in. A belief I desperately wanted to embrace again. Because getting drunk every night and screwing Gabe's friends wasn't making me feel a whole lot better. Penning Maria's name on the men's room wall at Rico's Tavern with a list of the sex services she offered at dirt-cheap prices hadn't really influenced Gabe's decision either.

As for magical, California was full to the brim with it. Californians practically invented pop culture. They were the leading bleeding edge in everything cool — except for New Yorkers, of course. The Bay Area offered me a new start out from beneath the shadow of my breakup with Gabe and my well-meaning parents handing me advice on what I should and shouldn't do. As an only child, I received my parent's high-beam attention, and the intensity proved overwhelming even at the best of times. In California, I could be anyone or anything I wanted to be. The main question I kept asking myself was: what did I *want* to be?

As my savings account dwindled, secondary questions became more important, such as where to find a job in a place where I knew almost nobody. Pretty difficult to appear perky and competent on a job interview with a migraine named Gabe Capellani lodged in my chest.

Nothing I did took the edge off that pain. I tried every medicine on the market: Sonoma Valley wine, pretty men, hashish, funny men, cocaine, brainy men, more wine, other pills I should never have let pass my lips. I missed appointments, failed to return recruiter's calls, slept until noon.

My life was a royal mess.

One day I skidded my battered Jetta into the parking lot at Goat Rock Beach by the mouth of Sonoma County's Russian River. I sat on that beach for hours, feeling the wind, smelling the sea, hearing the gulls, watching the seals fish. I felt oddly at home there, the ocean constantly murmuring like a friendly companion, the creatures coming and going about their business paying me no mind. I'd visited a lot of East Coast beaches, but never felt that same draw, the deep encompassing peace, that seemed to radiate from the Pacific.

Never been much of a nature person, but that summer nature became my medicine, a place where I finally belonged. I felt almost as if I must have lived there before. Something about the vista felt familiar, like an old memory. At the southern end of the beach, sat massive Goat Rock, an outcrop attached to the mainland by a narrow isthmus. Sounds funny, but me and that stubborn rock had a lot in common. Both standing alone against the tide. Both barely maintaining a hold on the continent. Both enduring everything life — or in the rock's case, the Pacific — had to throw at us.

That's what I did that first Sonoma summer. I endured. Until the pain in my chest didn't feel so debilitating. And I could step back onto life's carousel.

Turns out all the years I'd been managing accounts at Filene's had prepared me well for other office work. Guy Salvatore, the Parts Department Manager at Sonoma Diesel, hired me on the spot one blistering August afternoon. Guy was a fat, balding version of Gabe's uncle, Carlo, who leered at anything in a skirt, but thought the sun and moon rose in his wife's eyes. The work wasn't difficult, a little boring, but paid well. The arrangement worked for me. Except the migraine in my chest kept pulsing. No matter what I did, I couldn't forget Gabe.

Ordinarily, I could sort of see what made other people tick, their hopes and fears, their deep wishes, the way they fell hopelessly, helplessly in love. I intuitively knew how they felt. Hard to explain how exactly. But the one thing I couldn't get over was I hadn't recognized anything amiss with my own relationship. And now Gabe was merrily playing house with Maria, expecting a kid for God sakes, while I worked a corporate job three thousand miles away surrounded by attentive men I could care less about except for an occasional weekend in the hay, which — don't get me wrong

— was fun, but felt sort of hollow now that I knew what being in love really felt like.

So I plodded on, one day at a time, enjoying the men who spun through the revolving door of my life for a few days or months as the case might be. No idea how to fix my wounded heart. Or even *if* I could fix it. Nobody came close to competing with Gabe. I'd been so consumed, I hadn't paid attention, hadn't seen him slipping away. Now two years later I was still single, periodically pining away for a man who used to be mine, but wasn't any longer. A man married to my best friend from sixth grade. Fucker.

I kept telling myself one day I'd get over him. Time was supposed to be the all-powerful healer. My theory was Mr. Time had been asleep on the job for way too damn long.

Chapter Two

That September my best friend Jess who worked in the Sonoma Diesel Service Department found herself single too, but I had a suspicion that wouldn't last. The day the new shop foreman started, she phoned me, and the moment the words spilled out of her mouth, I knew her solo days would soon be over.

"He's an ass," she announced, her clipped voice unconvincingly irritated.

"He's definitely got a damn fine ass," I laughed, "I saw him getting out of his truck this morning when I drove in, so I stopped by and introduced my feisty self."

"Leave it to you, Ms. Garcia," Jess smothered a laugh.

"When I handed him my phone number, he acted all 'aw shucks ma'am', but I cut to the chase and told him his wedding ring wouldn't bother me none." I'd meant it too. Jay Green was just about the prettiest man I'd ever seen and I couldn't help imagining what his mustache would feel like against my neck. Really didn't matter to me whether he was married. I wasn't out to steal another woman's husband, just wanted to enjoy his charms for a while. But I could tell by the way he'd looked at me, I wasn't his type and he likely wouldn't take me up on the offer. Jess now was an entirely different matter.

"Reets! You didn't!" My friend always acted so shocked at my lack of demure femininity. Sometimes she was so old fashioned.

"Worth a try," I said. "Ooops, gotta go Jess. Dave Higgins just walked in, and I swear the Viking looks better than he did last week."

No one would ever call Dave Higgins a pretty man. Not by a long shot. But there was something about the man's wide shoulders and dishwater blond curls that made me feel like running my hands all over him just for fun. Or maybe I wanted to see what I might find beneath the flannel shirt and blue jeans.

"Customer, Reet," said Guy Salvatore, bringing my attention back to earth. His bushy brown eyebrows waggled at me, his teeth set in a ferocious grin. The man sensed something bubbling between Dave and I and filled in the rest with his dirty imagination. Some days I wished he wasn't so damn happily married.

"Got it," I said, climbing to my feet and yanking my emerald v-neck sweater slightly lower. I approached the counter, black skirt swaying.

Dave chewed the side of his lip, pretending to peruse one of the catalogs. He'd recently taken the Operations Manager position at Nowalk Transportation, helping refurbish and expand the truck fleet, so I'd seen a lot of him the past few months.

"Good morning, Dave," I smiled.

"Morning, Rita." he smiled back, green eyes wandering across my face, down the curves of my sweater and back up to my grin.

"Let me know if I can help you. I mean, if there's something you'd like to order up." I cocked my head and raised my painted eyebrows expectantly.

"Oh, I will. I definitely will." Dave chuckled.

I watched thoughts flit across his chiseled face. Typically, I could make a pretty good guess at those delicious thoughts, but I kept it professional and waited for him to direct the conversation. After all, I could be wrong. He could be in there just to buy gaskets or a water pump for one of Nowalk's trucks. But I was rarely wrong about men — at least not ones I wasn't head over heels in love with.

"Lemme ask you, Rita. Where you from? East Coast somewhere?" Dave's voice was calm and smooth, and he looked me right in the eye as if I mattered. His aftershave smelled like orange spice tea.

"New Yohk," I said, allowing my accent to flourish. "Moved here two years ago."

"Sounds like a story I'd like to hear. Come with me on a run up to Sacramento someday and fill me in." He motioned toward his red Chevy pickup with his chin. "Let me make you an offer you can't refuse."

"Mister, I don't even know you," I teased. But I wasn't all that alarmed by Dave's quasi-invitation. I had an eye for troublemakers and although he probably wasn't a Boy Scout, Dave didn't seem overtly dangerous — but he didn't strike me as someone who could be pushed around either. I studied him thoughtfully, wondering how far we'd make it down the highway before I wiggled my way onto his lap.

"Easy way to fix that," he said, his voice casual. He flipped pages in the parts catalog, dog-earing a few for future reference.

"Are you a magician by chance, Rita?" Dave asked, changing the subject. A frown creased his lips.

Momentarily confused, I looked into his serious eyes. His green irises were actually a combination of olive and golden brown, a color that reminded me of a sunny autumn day. "What makes you think that?"

"Because whenever I look at you everyone else disappears," Dave smiled. Then we both laughed. To his credit, his chuckle was self-conscious, as though he hadn't really meant to spin that corny line, at least not in such a public place. No one was there to hear it except me though, so he shrugged it off, looking almost like a teenager with a flush in his cheeks.

He hooked me then, although I don't think he knew it.

Deliberately snugging his navy blue baseball cap onto his blond curls, Dave turned and left without saying another word. He paused and grinned back at me from the door, a promise of sorts, then stepped out into the October sunshine. His blond hair turned gold in the morning light and for a moment I imagined his mead-drinking, knife-wielding ancestors storming some rocky shoreline.

Dave didn't need to say another word to me that morning. The bloody red B on his hat did the talking for him. The man was a damn Boston Red Sox fan and he'd worn that hat to flaunt it in my face. His self-satisfied grin should have made me angry. Because Boston fans made all New York Yankees fans want to slap the smirking grins off their stinking faces. Especially in October after the Beantown Bums stole the AL East crown. The old baseball rivalry ran deep in my veins. But somehow that morning, I wasn't angry. Instead, bold brawny Dave Higgins made me smile.

The man had cojones. I'd give him that. It had been a long time since I'd met someone as interesting as Dave. Smiling to myself, I returned to my desk and watched the red pickup leave the parking lot in a plume of dust.

"When's the hot date?" Guy Salvatore asked on his way to the coffeepot.

"Only a matter of time, Guy," I laughed. "Only a matter of time."

Chapter Three

My old friend Time must have taken a long lunch or something, because the next time I saw Dave Higgins almost a month had passed. A month where my friend Jess fell hopelessly in love with Jay Green and him with her, except she didn't want to admit it. She had this thing about dating married men, and even though word was Jay was in one of those "open" marriages, Jess still balked. Well, more than balked; she ran like a frightened fawn. But like I told her, she'd already fallen for the man, and once it happens, there's no getting that back in the box.

Anyway, Dave timed his next parts pickup at 4:45 pm the Friday before Thanksgiving. The Yankees had gone down in defeat in the playoffs and it was probably best he'd stayed away until I'd had a chance to calm the hell down. He strolled in the door right before I locked it, all casual-like, his Boston cap perched on his blond curls.

"Evening, Rita." His eyes crinkled into a smile as he took in my short purple skirt and oversize COOGI sweater, a mesmerizing tapestry of turquoise, apricot, and amethyst stripes and swirls.

"Evening, Dave." I peered up at him from beneath my eyelashes. I pulled the paperwork for his order, my hands automatically performing the familiar task while I studied his tanned face. Behind me I heard Guy harrumphing as he told the warehouseman to punch back in, and trolley Mr. Higgins' order out to his truck.

"Nice sweater. Colorful." Dave's voice was teasing, his dark green eyes merry.

"Yes, colorful. Like fabulous me," I offered, daring him to comment otherwise.

"Yes, exactly like fabulous you," he laughed. "Speaking of fabulous you, what are you up to tonight?"

"I'll need to check my calendar," I sniffed, pretending indifference, then pounded the staple gun on his paperwork with more oomph than necessary.

"Well, please do." Dave's voice thrummed in my ears, the low vibration barely discernible, but I could feel it in my hips. "I'd like to make you that offer you can't refuse."

"Really." I lifted my chin to look up at him. "And you expect me to agree. Just like that." I

221

snapped my fingers to punctuate the "that." I was a little miffed he'd waited so long to ask me out. In fact, I'd begun to think I'd read Dave's interest wrong.

"Well," he said, confidence wavering slightly in the face of my pushback, "I'd hoped you might join me for a pizza tonight. At that Olivetti's place everyone's talking about."

Pursing my apricot lips, I considered the man in front of me. Not gorgeous. Not necessarily smart. But I liked him. I knew the invitation to dinner was no way just about dinner. What Dave didn't know for certain, was I OK with that.

More than OK with that.

"Come on. Take a chance on me," he said, holding out his calloused hand. "Grab your purse and coat. You won't regret it." His smile promised an interesting evening.

My return smile promised something more than interesting.

Game for an Olivetti's pizza and whatever else Dave had in mind, I placed my hand in his outstretched palm. I think the electric shock that accompanied the touch surprised both of us, so much so, that the moment we were safely ensconced in the truck cab, he pulled me against him and kissed me long and hard without wasting any time on small talk.

No frills, no games. Just Dave and me. To describe my reaction as enthusiastic would be an understatement. I think both of us were so completely astounded by our intense chemistry we couldn't have put the brakes on if we wanted. Pent-up tension ruled our responses, as if we were high school kids who hadn't learned the definition of self-control. Except there was nothing high school about Dave. Or me. And we both knew it.

"Woman, you are like fire," he gasped, his hands roaming freely.

"You're goddamn right," I said unbuckling his belt. "What are you gonna do about it?"

Shoving the seat as far back as it would go, he grabbed me by the waist and settled me on his lap. He nestled one hand up under my skirt, his expert fingers brushing parts of my anatomy that made me breathlessly squirm.

"Don't be in too much of a hurry, lovely Rita" he warned, laughing.

"Don't make me hurry, then," I warned back, staring into his smiling eyes.

"You want to stop?" His voice teased me the same way his fingers did.

"Better not if you know what's good for you," I growled, my body doing its talking against his.

"Oh, I know what's good for me Ms. Meter. And right now, you're the best thing I've had on my lap all goddamn year."

"Do tell, Mr. Higgins," I said, my voice husky.

Dave's lips found my neck. We stopped talking then, the business between us more consuming than words, a language of touch that superseded anything we could frame into sentences.

Thankfully sunset in November came early and the parking lot was vacant.

Sometime later, Dave brushed the hair back from my face and kissed me on the forehead. "How about that pizza, lovely Rita?"

"You aren't gonna call me that all the time now are you?" Aware of the Beatles reference, I climbed off his lap and gathered my purse from the truck floor to search for my hairbrush.

"I might. But only if you let me tow you away for tea again later tonight," Dave smiled, turning the truck key. "When the spirit moves me."

"Spirit, huh?" I laughed, thinking the type of spirit that moved him earlier had one powerful drive.

"Spirit," he confirmed, laughing. "There's more where that came from, you know."

"Really?" I pitched my voice to mimic an incredulous thirteen year-old. "You'll have to show me."

"Don't worry, I will," Dave said. "After pizza and a drink or two at the Riverrun Tavern where my friend Jim Mason and his band are playing tonight."

"Promises, promises," I teased, running my hand up his leg.

"You have no idea what I have in mind for you, lady," he smiled. "But first I need food."

Olivetti's Pizzeria was packed, a line forming in the flagstone foyer to await an open table. I didn't want to wait, but didn't have a better dinner idea either. Gazing around the dark-paneled restaurant, I suddenly saw Jess sitting by herself in a booth. Just my luck.

"Jessica Carline!" I waved, then grabbed Dave by the hand and dodged my way between tables. Sliding into the seat opposite Jess, I winked and yanked my grinning date down beside me. With a wide silly smile like that, everyone who saw us together would instantly know what we'd been doing in his truck.

Keeping my voice cool, I smiled. "Mind if we join you? Dave, you know Jess, right?"

"Sure do," Dave said, his chiseled Viking features looking almost handsome in the muted lighting.

"Wow. Yeah. Well, HI!" Jess stumbled her way through the words, uncomfortably surprised to see us. Making a guess it had something to do with men — didn't it always? — I recalled seeing an orange Chevy pickup in the parking lot. She was probably there with her old boyfriend Kevin and didn't want anyone to know they were back together yet.

"You here with Kevie Mac? I saw his truck out in the parking lot." I cocked my head toward Jess, then snuggled up against Dave's side. Thinking about what we'd been doing an hour earlier made my legs feel like jelly. His fingers creeping up the inside of my thigh beneath the table didn't exactly keep my mind from wandering either.

"No. Actually I'm here with a friend." Jess said, her dark eyes suddenly troubled. She gazed around the restaurant like a nervous colt. Probably looking for Kev.

"Hi, Rita," Jay Green said, plunking two beers on the table and sitting his tight backside on the seat beside Jess. "How's it, Dave?"

For the second time that evening, I was surprised nearly out of my skin. Jess and Jay were here together? What the hell?

Dave, on the other hand, took the news in stride. "Good to see ya, Jay," he said, extending his huge hand.

Jay grasped the outstretched palm and shook it warmly as if it were old home week. "So what's good here, Jess? I was looking at that Meatsa...."

Dinner was fun. More than fun, actually. With a foursome, I found out way more about Dave than I imagined I would. His humor was entertaining, a blast of oxygen, and I couldn't help feeling there was the potential for something more to develop between us. It was something I hadn't felt about anyone for a long damn time and I stuffed the sentiment away. It wouldn't do to kindle any expectations.

Enjoy the moment, I told myself, even though I knew he could just stand up and shrug and leave any time without apology. Yeah, I'd be hurt, but there were no promises between us. Not really. Besides, it was too way soon for anything like that.

His hunting story about a goose who refused to be retrieved by his dog, Duke, had us all in stitches. The goose had apparently pecked the dog ruthlessly on the nose the previous Sunday, scared the bejeezus out of the poor thing, and sent it scurrying under the truck with his tail tucked.

"Call the dog shrink!" I declared. "You're gonna need professional help if you ever want that dog to retrieve anything ever again."

"I think it's too soon to tell whether there's any permanent mental damage," Dave said with a perfectly straight face.

Then he said something that made me know he and I weren't done quite yet.

"But I'll keep your recommendation in mind, Ms. Meter." The Viking smiled down at me, his green-gold eyes nearly glowing. I remembered his after-pizza promise and found myself blushing.

I hardly ever blush. I'm typically the one who instigates blushing. With this man, the shoe was on the other foot. I wasn't sure I liked that yet.

"Ms. Meter?" Jess raised an eyebrow.

"Lovely Rita Meter Maid," Dave smiled, then waggled his bushy blonde eyebrows. "May I inquire discretely. When are you free to have some fun with me?"

His fingertips brushed higher up my thigh, quivering dangerously close to where they'd been in the truck, making it clear what type of fun he had in mind. I wondered briefly if we'd make it out to the parking lot before I managed to control my desire to.... Reigning my one-track mind back from the edge, I batted my eyelashes while Jess and Jay laughed at Dave's twist on the Beatles lyrics.

"We're headed down to the Riverrun Tavern tonight. You guys should come. Jim Mason Band is playing." I posed the invitation, then intertwined my manicured fingers with Dave's rough ones to stop his exploring digits from going any further. Any higher and I'd melt onto the floor.

"Oh thanks, but I don't think—" Jess said.

"Jim Mason? From up Redding way?" Jay interrupted.

Chapter Four

An hour later, the four of us were seated in a fake leather booth at the Riverrun Tavern, beers all around, listening to Jim's band perform some classic Country Western hits. Stories about love and loss that could rip your heart out or make you laugh. I'd never listened to C&W artists much because I was more of a rock-n-roll connoisseur, but I found it had a depth I hadn't imagined and the storytelling hit home. Real life; real people.

Jess and Jay left hand-in-hand mid-way through the second set. I watched them leave without saying goodbye, knowing what happened next was one of those inevitable events written in the stars. I wasn't a psychologist or anything; but I didn't need a college degree to recognize their deep connection, however much Jess might wish it otherwise.

"I think that there's a done deal," said Dave, smiling down at me as our friends disappeared through the crowd.

"I think you're right," I said, kissing him on the lips.

"I think you and I are about to be moved again by the spirit, lovely Rita." He kissed me back, letting it linger.

"What are we waiting for?" I murmured.

Laughing, he stood and drew me to my feet. "I have plans for you, my lady," he said, gathering me into his arms. Then he stooped and swung his muscled arm against the back of my knees and lifted me off my feet. Jim Mason caught sight of us and stopped the song, his long hand held palm out.

"You go, Dave," Jim said into the microphone as all eyes in the dark club peered in our direction.

"I'm a-going, Jimbo," Dave shouted over his shoulder.

"Looks like old Dave's found someone he likes," Jim chuckled, as did the rest of the audience.

We left the good-natured laughter behind and made our escape out into the cool November night. Stars glimmered in the heavens behind the moonrise, casting dim shadows across the earth. River fog coalesced, spreading a fine cloak of mist around the cottonwoods at the edge of the gravel parking lot.

"Jim might be right, Ms. Meter," Dave mumbled as he packaged me safely in the front seat of his truck. Then he drove us out to his place in Glen

Ellen where he showed me exactly what he'd been planning all evening. Breathless, I squirmed as his lips and fingers found their way to spots that had been neglected for way too long.

I fell asleep wrapped in his strong arms thinking a dangerous thought. *I could get used to this man.*

The next morning I awoke naked in Dave's empty bed, my body pleasantly sore in places I'd forgotten existed. The smell of coffee and bacon drew me into the country kitchen, where the tall half-naked Scandinavian held a folded newspaper in his large hand as he stared out the window at the live oaks bordering the creek behind his cabin.

"Mornin', lady," Dave smiled, "Coffee?"

"Please." I sat unselfconsciously topless at the white tile breakfast bar, my fingers curled around the warm mug he handed me. I took a long sip, enjoying the strong taste and the view — both the live oaks and the broad-shouldered man studying the Wall Street Journal.

"Stocks," he explained, flipping the newspaper onto the counter.

"You invest?" I tried to keep the surprise out of my voice. That a man who drove truck for a living would know anything about investments made him all the more intriguing.

"I do."

"How's the market treating you?"

"So far, good. Got some money on a technology company in Canada, a coffee company in Seattle, and a cereal company in Michigan. One stock split last year, another one looks set to do the same. And I have my eye on a windmill company in Oregon."

"You ever do any investing?" Dave studied me appreciatively, his attention firmly fixed on my naked breasts.

"No, but I'd be interested to give it a try if someone would—"

"Do you always walk around half-naked?" he interrupted, rounding the breakfast bar to kiss me good morning. He tasted like coffee and cinnamon toothpaste and smelled like mint soap. His fingertips casually tickled their way down to my nipples.

"Only in a house where all the people walk around half-naked." I countered, moving my warm hands around his backside. "I'm feeling moved by the spirit," I murmured as he groaned with pleasure. "How about you?"

"You are going to wear me out, darlin', but I'll die a happy, happy man." He buried his fingers in my hair and kissed me thoroughly, all the way back to bed.

Just enjoy the moment, I told myself. *Right now is all you have.*

See, I had to tell myself those things, so I wouldn't care too terribly much when Dave found someone else. Because I had to face the fact that whatever we had going probably wouldn't last. I simply wasn't what folks called a keeper. I learned that little lesson from Gabe Capellani.

No way I was making the mistake of falling in love again. It just hurt too damn much

No way, I told myself. As if my words made any difference to my heart.

Chapter Five

The first Saturday in December, Dave picked me up in his truck for an outing he promised I would enjoy. Removing a blue and white bandana from his pocket, he dangled it in the air and smiled a mischievous smile.

"May I?" He folded the cloth kitty-corner into a headband.

"May you what?" I eyed the bandana, not liking where things appeared to be going one bit.

"I'd like this destination to be a sort of a surprise. Will you play along?"

Dave's voice sounded earnest, so I relented. "How long will I have to wear it?"

"Thirty minutes tops," he promised, placing it gently across my eyes and tying it at the back of my head.

"Okay, but no funny business." I harrumphed loudly, crossing my arms in front of my chest.

Dave started the truck and sniffed a laugh. "I hadn't considered funny business an option, but now that you mention it, sounds like fun." I felt his hand creeping under my sweatshirt.

"No!" I said, swatting at the hand, but finding only air. "I meant it."

"Alright already, lady. Keep your shorts on. Let's see who we have on the stereo." Dave turned up *Sergeant Pepper's Lonely Hearts Club Band* and sang enthusiastically to almost every song, starting with McCartney's "When I'm Sixty Four" all the way through Starr's "With a Little Help from My Friends."

"Would you believe in a love at first sight?" he sang, his low voice slightly off-tune.

"Yes, I'm certain that it happens all the time," I sang the return line softly.

"Me too," Dave said, turning off the truck. "Open your eyes. We're here."

I removed the bandana and blinked in the weak sunlight. Tall sand dunes ruled the landscape as far as the eye could see.

"We're going that way," Dave pointed to a path that bisected two of the smallest dunes. "Okay with you?"

"Let's go." I opened the truck door and smelled the salty air, smiling. "I love the ocean."

"Yeah?" He draped his arm across my shoulder. "I didn't know that." Dave's black Labrador Retriever, Duke, ran ahead of us, his keen nose lifted into the wind.

"Now you do," I smiled. We followed a well-worn path through the grass-speckled dunes, emerging onto a long sand beach. Waves crashed against the shore, the familiar beat vibrating an ancient rhythm deep in my bones. To the south, tall cliffs held against the pounding surf. To the north, gold sand meandered between a pair of towering stone spires, reminding me of my beloved Goat Rock. Terns screeched their greetings, riding the air currents out to sea and back again. Sandpipers scoured the gold-brown sand, long beaks searching for a bite of breakfast.

The shoreline was dotted with ocean debris: smooth sand dollars, bits of crab shells, weathered bones, and seashells in various colors and sizes. I found a few abalone shell shards, the wet turquoise and violet hues shining bright in the winter light. All around us the beach shared its treasure: driftwood carved by the sea into the shape of an old woman's face, a red and purple jellyfish that smelled like rot that neither Dave now I dared touch, a horseshoe crab shell, a red-tailed hawk feather. Duke pattered between us, sniffing everything, barking at birds, then rushing periodically into the surf to fetch the water-logged sticks Dave tossed for him.

For lunch, we sat shoulder-to-shoulder with our backs to a huge log, sheltered from the cool wind.

"Tuna fish?" Dave asked, removing two wrapped sandwiches from his backpack.

"Perfect," I grinned, appreciating his forethought.

Handing me a bottle of water, we ate in companionable silence while Duke continued his exploratory excursions through the scrub grass bordering the sand dunes.

"So, tell me what you want to be when you grow up, Dave." I took his hand in mine, studying the lines and calluses in his palms.

Duke rushed by us dragging a stick the size of a small log. "He's gonna wear his teeth out on that thing," Dave laughed, then he turned his attention to me. "Hmmmm... well, since you asked, that's a question I've thought about my whole life. At first, I wanted to be a career soldier, until I found out I wasn't cut out for all the bureaucracy."

Dave grinned. "Then, when I got out of the service and moved back to Redding, it was all about driving truck for my dad's company, learning the business to take it over one day." He grabbed the end of Duke's long stick and began a tug-of-war, the dog scrambling madly in the soft sand. A rumbling growl emanated from deep in the animal's throat. "He thinks he's so tough," Dave hissed, swishing the stick side-to-side

"Anyway, I knew I wasn't the sharpest tool in the shed. And apparently my dad did too. After all the time I'd spent in the Army, he'd gotten used to the idea my younger brother would take over the business instead of me. Wanted me to stay on the road. Drivin'. Said that was what I was best at.

Could have bowled me over with a feather when he told me." Releasing the stick, Dave let Duke scamper away with the win.

"I took this job with Nowalk hoping it might be a stepping stone to running my own fleet some day. I know I could do it, Rita. I've driven truck, so I know the challenges at the ground floor level. I've repaired machinery, bought and sold 'em, cannibalized 'em for parts when they finally outlasted their usefulness. I know a little bit about the business end, negotiating contracts and such. But there's a lot more to learn. I'm hoping Nowalk expands the way he's talked about and picks me to run his new office. He's hinted at it... I just don't know if I have the patience to wait until things come together. Or maybe I should look elsewhere? I dunno, Reets.

"What about you?" he countered. "What do you want to be when you grow up?"

"Do I have to grow up?" I teased, deflecting the question.

"I like that answer," Dave smiled. "I like it a lot, in fact." He shook his head, chuckling. "But I'm curious. Humor me."

Shrugging, I tipped my chin toward the sky. "When I moved out here three years ago, I had a boatload of time to think about that question. I was making a new start in a new place. I could remake myself into anything I wanted." I paused, thoughtful about what I wanted to say. "Funny thing was I found I didn't have the energy to remake myself right then. So, I did what we all do. One foot in front of the other. Brick by brick I built a new life for myself, made a few good friends. Fell into a job I found I really liked. All things considered, I was lucky." I watched a hawk soaring above the cliffs, her cry screeching across the sky. "So when you ask me that question today, the first thing that comes to mind is that I'd want to go further in my career, wherever that road takes me. I think I could be management material somewhere. Not at Sonoma Diesel obviously, because Guy Salvatore will probably never retire, but maybe somewhere else." I turned to find Dave watching me, a bemused expression on his face.

"I rarely hear women talk about their careers first. Most gals seem fixed on marriage and children and all that domestic stuff." Dave waved his hand in the air.

"Yeah, well, not really in the equation for me," I laughed. "I don't think I have the patience for kids."

"I hear that," Dave smiled. "Doesn't mean it might not happen someday."

"No. It doesn't. But I don't think that could ever be enough for me, you know? Too boring. Like you, business intrigues me. What makes one company thrive and another tank? Like the stocks you suggested I invest in. How did you know?"

"I didn't do all that well in school, but Economics made sense to me." Dave shrugged.

239

"Can't explain it. I read about the companies and then I pick. So far, so good."

"Damn right," I said, considering my quickly growing portfolio. "You're on to something. I like your goal, Mr. Higgins," I smiled. "I think you'd be good at running the show somewhere."

"Well thank you Ms. Meter. I appreciate that. And back at ya. You've got a good head on your shoulders and one of these days the right opportunity is going to knock on your door." Standing suddenly, he offered a hand to help me to my feet, then pulled me against him. "Speaking of which, I have a few management plans in mind for you this evening, my lady."

"Do tell," I said, smiling up at him.

Holding hands, we began the walk back to the truck, Duke dutifully dragging the same long stick behind us.

"I don't know how I'm going to convince him to leave the damn thing here." Dave cast a glance in Duke's direction.

"Maybe you don't need to. We could throw it in the back of the truck. Bring it with..."

"We could..." he said, thoughtful. "You are entirely too soft-hearted when it comes to that dog."

"You were saying something about plans?" I asked, bringing the conversation back on topic.

"Right. Well there's a bandana involved."

"You think I'm going to put that bandana back on?" I asked, incredulous.

240

"I can pretty much guarantee it." Dave waggled his eyebrows. "And frosting. Definitely frosting."

"Frosting?" I laughed.

"Yeah, you know, like you put on cake. Strawberry's my favorite." He eyed me like a luscious dessert, his lips twisting into a mischievous smile.

Later that evening, Dave and I sat atop his breakfast bar in the moonlight sipping chardonnay. Dusk had darkened to night and the house was filled with shadows. The countertop television cast a blue glow across the tile, tiny men chasing a small black biscuit across an ice rink, the Boston Bruins beating the stuffing out of the New York Islanders.

Dave slipped his arm across my shoulder and drew me against his chest. "I could get used to you living here with me, Rita," he whispered. The rain began, the pattering sound a soothing refrain against the metal roof.

"What do you see when you turn out the lights?" I whispered into his ear.

Dave slid off the counter and gathered me into his arms. "I can't tell you, but I know it's mine," he muttered the return line. Then he let me slide the blue and white bandana over his eyes so I could kiss him all over. Again.

Chapter Six

The rest of December passed like a whirlwind. The magical mystery tour of my life had somehow resurrected itself in the arms of a tall blond Viking who seemed to think I was the most fabulous thing since the Beatles. I was wined and dined and treated like a queen, and yet a part of me kept expecting it to end in a fiery blaze. Periodically I'd reign my pessimistic thoughts back, determined to allow someone else into my heart and dispel Gabe's ghost for good.

The Saturday before Christmas I left Dave asleep in the early dawn darkness and drove out to Goat Rock. Light drizzle peppered my windshield as I pulled my Jetta into the parking lot. Waves pummeled the beach as the Pacific high tide swelled inland. Donning my flannel-lined raincoat, I stepped out into the cold wind. My dark hair flew behind me in a tangled mass as I made my way down onto the sand, the mist caressing my face as the sky lightened. I sat on a seat-sized rock, drinking in the smell and sound of the ocean, inviting the wind and rain to wash my cares away. Letting myself simply be.

As morning broke, I watched the world change as I had so many times before, the play of light on the gray-green water, the striations of color on the wet stones, stalwart Goat Rock still enduring everything the Pacific threw at her. I'd come to clear my mind, to make a decision.

Dave had officially asked me to move in with him and I owed him an answer. Part of me wanted to beat feet home to my apartment, pack my things, and rush back into his arms. The other part of me screamed caution; I'd only known him six weeks.

Things that seemed too good to be true usually were. I didn't want to be a fool again for love, didn't want to get unceremoniously dumped on my ass when Dave found another woman who caught his eye.

We'd talked about our respective histories. He'd insisted we get it all out in the open one Saturday night when he took me to dinner at Fisherman's Wharf in San Francisco. Didn't want there to be secrets between us. I hadn't particularly wanted to talk about it at the time, but it seemed important to him. After we did, I felt like we were closer, that our relationship was more real.

Funny what a difference real makes.

That Saturday night San Francisco Bay reflected the city lights beneath a nearly full moon. Dave's familiarity with the restaurant menu and wait staff surprised me. Obviously it wasn't his first time there. The waiter greeted him as "Mr. Dave" with a twinkling fatherly eye.

"And this is Ms. Rita." Dave introduced me, while the waiter bowed over my hand with a charming smile.

"Wonderful to meet you, Ms. Rita. May I suggest the Lobster Newberg tonight, sir?"

"You may," Dave smiled. "OK by you?"

"Sounds wonderful. Thank you," I nodded.

When the waiter left, Dave held his wine glass aloft. "A toast."

"Okay." I lifted my glass to meet his, curious to hear what he'd say.

"To us," he proposed.

"To us," I agreed. We clinked the crystal long-stemmed glasses together, the ring a pleasant celebratory sound.

"Tell me your story, Rita. I want to know everything about you." Dave looked at me intently.

"Well, that's a tall order," I chuckled, masking the nervousness pulsing through my veins. The cherry red spaghetti strap dinner dress suddenly felt tight against my chest, making it difficult to draw breath. I didn't know what to say, what to tell him. What I wanted to tell him. Besides, what if he didn't like what he heard? What if he decided he didn't like me at all?

"Please," he said, grasping my free hand in his. "I know practically nothing about you. But what I do know is that I want to know you."

"You sure about that?" I looked away. Maybe I couldn't do this relationship thing. Maybe I didn't actually want to. That was OK. I could do one night stands. One weekend stands even.

"Hey, where'd you go there?" Dave squeezed my hand.

"Nowhere," I fumbled. "It's just...I don't want you to think...."

"How 'bout I go first then? I'll show you my dirty laundry then you show me yours?" Grinning, Dave fearlessly dove into the deep end.

I sat and listened, my fingers intertwined with his. He talked about meeting his wife Gina in Georgia right before he was discharged from the Army and falling madly, deeply in love with her, marrying her in Las Vegas, bringing her home to Redding, a town she hated on first sight. To his dismay, the marriage began crumbling almost immediately. Then Jay and Candy moved up from Texas and things really came apart. Falling for Candy was something he hadn't expected, and although the affair lasted almost three years, he regretted it.

"She was my best friend's wife for God sakes. And I just...I dunno. Gina was unhappy. I was unhappy and didn't know how to fix the marriage or end it. I just wanted to be around someone who wasn't such a downer. And Candy...well, Candy can be mighty persuasive."

"Persuasive?" I cocked my head and looked him in the eye. "Define persuasive."

"Well...kind of like how you can be mighty persuasive, Rita," Dave blushed.

"She's a good fuck," I summarized. "And probably quite pretty. That kind of persuasive?"

"You got me there." Dave stared out the window. "I ain't proud to admit it, but it's the truth. Beyond bed we never had much in common. She ain't interested in sports or the stock market or the trucking business or any of the things that make my world tick. Never asked about my work, like you do. She was lonely, I guess. And I was willing and available. Like I said, ain't proud of fucking my buddy's wife, but then when Jay and Gina took up together, I thought, you know, tit for tat. Hoped it was one of those — whatta ya call it — "mutually beneficial" arrangements."

"What ended it? Who ended it?" I asked, curious what had driven them to break it off.

"In a way Gina was the one who ended it for all of us. She told us all to fuck off one weekend, packed a suitcase, and went home to Georgia. I ended things with Candy a few months after Gina left town. Had a come-to-Jesus meeting with myself and pondered some tough questions. Sounds funny to say now, but I figured out I was bored driving truck. Needed a change. Don't get me wrong, Candy was still quite persuasive...." Dave smiled and shrugged. "But after Gina left I became determined to do something with my life. Get the hell out of Redding. Make a new start. I jumped at this opportunity with Nowalk last summer, and, as luck would have it, Jay accepted that foreman's position at Sonoma Diesel shortly after. So, we're living in the same county again. Go figure."

Dave looked at me, green eyes serious. "I ain't interested in Candy anymore, Rita. I see Jay every once in a while when I catch a beer at the Riverrun after work, but I rarely see his wife." His rough calloused fingertips gently rubbed the top of my knuckles. "She can't hold a candle to you, lady."

Unbidden tears welled behind my eyelids. Dave's unquestionable sincerity dispelled some of the immobilizing fear I felt at sharing my own story. I nodded, speechless for a moment. Then, managing a weak smile, I took a deep breath. "I guess it's my turn now... I met Gabriel Capellani at a nightclub in Queens...."

The sound of gulls calling brought me back to the present moment. The rain had subsided, but the wind still lashed the waves, spray flying high into the air. I hadn't said good-bye to Gabe. Never thought I could or would. But maybe it was time.

"Hear that, Gabe," I said aloud, "I'm finally saying good-bye."

Out in the bay, the rain began again, a curtain of water moving toward land with the prevailing wind. A moment later the deluge reached me, instantly soaking my hair to the scalp. Laughing, I stood and pin wheeled my arms, feeling the tendrils of cool moist air slip through my fingers. Then I turned and ran back to the car, no closer to a decision whether to move in with Dave than when I'd arrived, but somehow lighter.

Chapter Seven

By Christmas Eve, I'd formed a plan, a compromise of sorts. I couldn't really give up my apartment —mostly because I still had six months on the lease that I renewed after my cousin Jackie's expired and didn't want to screw up my credit. But if I was really honest with myself, it was mostly because if Dave and I didn't work out, I'd still have a fallback. I knew it was my old Gabe wound making me hesitate before jumping in with both feet, but I couldn't seem to help it. I wanted a trial subscription so to speak, a way to try out living with Dave without getting all wrapped around the axle about where I'd live if we decided to call it quits. I was going to tell Dave I'd move in with him that night, wrap it up in a present with a bow, so to speak.

Late that afternoon, I packed a suitcase with a change of clothes and a bottle of wine. Then I pinned my shoulder-length curls up into a clip with tiny ringlets framing my face and took extra care with my makeup — lots of dark eye shadow to ensure the sultriest look possible. My outfit was simple: a garter belt with black fishnet stockings, an oversized golden Christmas bow affixed to my hair clip, and my long black Italian leather coat cinched closed at the waist. I figured opening this particular Christmas present — namely me — would be a largely experiential gift for Dave. I'd give him the watch I bought later, after he'd had some time to play with his first present.

Smiling to myself, I pointed the Jetta down the highway to Glen Ellen. When I arrived at Dave's property, I parked my car out by the main road and walked down the dirt drive to the cabin, black high heels wobbling on the uneven ground beneath the giant live oaks. My plan was that since he wouldn't hear me arrive, he wouldn't know I was there until I knocked. He'd open the door to discover his mystery guest. I couldn't wait to see his face when I opened my coat and let it drop around my feet.

As I approached the house, I found Jay's blue Ford pickup in the driveway beside Dave's red Chevy. Dave hadn't said anything about company tonight, otherwise, I would have dressed for the occasion. Standing in the inky darkness beneath one of the huge oak limbs, I watched the house, trying to decide what to do next. I could return to my car and change into some suitable clothing, but...why would Dave invite Jay over Christmas Eve without telling me?

Colored Christmas lights sparkled in the windows, a kaleidoscope of reds and greens and sunny golds. A tendril of wood smoke spiraled out of the stone chimney. The porch held a collection of boots and dog toys, two rattan chairs casting shadows against the wooden planks. This was a warm and welcoming home that could be mine tomorrow.

So why was I standing outside in the dark? Why was I hesitating?

The answer became all too clear as a man and a woman moved into view in the picture window. The man was Dave, dark blond hair askew, a red and white checkered dish towel over his shoulder. The woman was a pretty platinum blonde in a form-fitting red velvet dress. Candace Green.

Curious, I moved to the side of the house next to the window, hoping Duke would not hear me and start barking. I watched Dave and Candy converse, then began hearing snippets of words.

"I thought... Christmas...." The woman's soft Southern accent wafted through the pane glass.

"Candycane. How...girls ... why tonight? " I could only catch one word out of three, but Dave's mumbled voice sounded irritated.

"Jay's head over heels in love with his fucking secretary. Like you didn't know." Candy's voice rang sharp now, her anger bubbling to the surface. Interesting she'd be pissed at Jess, but why the hell was she here at Dave's?

"... still... I thought you wanted to make this open marriage deal work? You leave your family Christmas Eve because you're miffed at the man for something you've done to him how many times?"

Hearing Dave tell Candy what for made me smile, but then I saw her hands traveling up his chest. She licked her deep red lips, deliberately seductive. Her voice went all soft and warm like honey. "I do want to make it work.... that's why I thought...." Her words faded as she stood on her tiptoes and placed her lips on his. Candy's long blonde hair cascaded down her back, her lithe fingers coming to rest on Dave's belt buckle. Dave's huge hands moved to her shapely waist.

I didn't watch what happened next. Couldn't bring myself to play a voyeur to a man I'd foolishly fallen in love with despite everything inside warning me to never do it again. Part of me wanted to storm in and rake my nails across the woman's pretty face, the other part felt ashamed I'd been gullible enough to believe Dave fancied me. In that moment I simply wanted to escape somewhere I'd never have to see him again. Eyes filling with hot tears, I treaded silently back down the driveway into the night.

The drive home passed in a blur. I thought about heading out to Goat Rock, but then decided to grab a warmer coat and a corkscrew to open the wine bottle. Hell, while I was at it, I'd grab a second bottle. Why not?

As I mounted the steps to my apartment, I noticed my Tiffany stained glass lamp glowing bright in my front window. I never kept that lamp lit when I left home. Never. When I approached the apartment door, I saw a shadow move across the curtains.

Someone was in my house.

This night was just getting better and better by the moment. First my boyfriend taking up with his old flame, then someone robbing my apartment. Merry fucking Christmas.

Suddenly spitting angry, I quietly tried the door handle. Unlocked. Then I kicked the door all the way open, slamming it against the interior wall, ready to scream bloody murder. Instead, the intruder herself screamed, dropped a full beer bottle onto the beige living room carpet, and skittered up onto my leather couch her dark eyes wide.

"Jackie?" I said, staring at the woman.

"God damn it, Rita. You scared the crap out of me." Indignant now, my cousin scampered into the kitchen to grab a towel to sop up the beer spill, her long black skirt flaring behind her.

"What the hell are you doing here?" I gasped, stumbling to a kitchen chair and leaning my throbbing head in my hands on the glass tabletop. My heart beat slowed as I breathed deeply, trying to find some calm in the storm of adrenaline and emotion whirling inside me. Gazing up at my cousin, I raised my eyebrows, awaiting the answer to my question. Why was Jackie in Santa Rosa on Christmas Eve instead of Santa Cruz?

"I could ask you the same thing." Jackie's dark brown eyes took in the crinkled bow on my head and the fishnet stockings. "Looks like you were on your way to one hot party. What happened? You look a mess, girlfriend."

"Look who's talking," I said, nodding at my cousin's wrinkled black silk attire, the low cut bodice revealing her charms. "You drive up this afternoon?"

"Damn right I did," Jackie spit. "Son of a bitch springs the news on me at brunch today. He's flying out to spend Christmas with his daughters in Vail. Skiing. *'Sorry Jacks... maybe you can join us next year after my divorce is final...'* Fucking asshole."

My cousin retrieved two fresh beers from the refrigerator and motioned toward the sofa. "Care to join me in getting shitfaced drunk?"

"Don't mind if I do," I said, stripping the hairclip and ridiculous golden bow off my head. "Meet you on the couch after I put on something decent." I kicked off my shoes and stood, noticing Jackie's designer suitcase beneath the table.

"What happened, Reets?" Jackie asked, her dark eyes concerned.

"Don't matter," I scoffed, and turned away. "Not anymore."

I knew she'd get the story out of me eventually. I simply hoped I could tell it without dissolving into a gooey mess.

Chapter Eight

The following morning I awoke to the phone ringing relentlessly beside my aching head. I picked up the receiver and plunked it down to stop the noise. My eyes felt like they'd been scrubbed with sandpaper and my head pounded with a headache I refused to call a hangover. Before I could make it to the bathroom, the phone rang again.

"What!" I said into the receiver, my voice sounding like a rasping frog.

"There you are," said Dave. "Honey, I was worried sick. 'Bout ready to head on over and check on you. Everything OK?"

"Fine. I'm fine. No need to check on me. I'm good." How I found the wherewithal to string together that many words was nothing short of miraculous.

"I missed you last night, babe. Fell asleep waiting...." Dave paused for my explanation, or perhaps my apology.

I felt no need to offer either, but settled on nipping further conversation in the bud with a firm good-bye. I'd never found the strength to say good-bye to Gabe; I'd been too much in love to imagine a life without him, so I'd hung on to the dream well after it ended. I knew now that decision hadn't been altogether healthy for me and I wasn't going to make that mistake again. Because I knew I'd never be OK with a guy who cheated on me behind my back...and with Dave I was already too far downstream to return to a light and breezy roll-in-the-hay relationship.

I'd screwed up and fallen in love with the Viking, damn it. The thing is, I thought that was what he wanted too. I thought he wanted us to be exclusive, which was why he'd asked me to move in with him. And like a damn fool, I'd been ready and willing to give him that. But all Candy had to do was crick her pretty little finger and be her "persuasive" self and it was all dashed on the rocks.

"Changed my mind," I said, keeping it short and sweet.

"Whadda ya mean, changed your mind?" Dave's words were spoken slow, his voice tentative.

"Let's cut to the chase, Dave. I'm saying good-bye. Don't call me anymore."

"Rita, hang on a second... What the hell—"

I didn't give him a chance to finish his sentence. "See you around." I promptly ended the call and unplugged the phone from the wall, the lump in my throat burning like hell.

"I guess you told him," Jackie said, leaning against the hallway doorframe with a towel wrapped around her torso.

"Yup. My turn to hit the shower. Coffee's in the cabinet beside the stove."

An hour later Jackie and I sat sipping our second cup of coffee together in the living room. All things considered, we were in a pretty sad state — on Christmas morning no less — although we both looked fabulous. It was one of those things women in our family did: when you were feeling like crap, you dressed impeccably and did not leave the bathroom mirror without perfect hair and makeup. I think it was an ingrained coping mechanism, a way to feel good about yourself despite the fact your life was spinning down the shitter.

"So, what are you going to do, Jacks?" I peered at my older cousin out of the corner of my eye.

Suddenly grinning, Jackie looked out the window at the cloud-streaked sky. "I think I'm booking a ticket to Vail, Colorado to take ski lessons from one of those handsome former Olympians."

"Brilliant." I smiled. "And I wonder who you might see there?"

"Don't matter," she shrugged, her curled dark hair bouncing on her shoulders. "You think with all the partying Christmas crowd I'm going to be spending too much time all by my lonesome? My friend Virginia offered me the couch in her condo, and she and her fiancé aren't staying more than a few days, so I'll have the place all to myself and whoever I decide to play with."

"You are an evil woman, Jackie." I grinned, knowing that once my cousin's boyfriend caught sight of her, he'd make sure the only one Jackie was playing with was him. Carl adored her, but he hadn't fully worked out his complicated divorce and was being extra careful not to upset his children by including his new partner in family gatherings until all was said and done.

"Let's see what the cards say about that, shall we?" Jackie jumped up and headed toward the spare room, her red rayon pantsuit flowing around her curves. "I'll have to do something about this stuff you're storing for me one of these days, Reets. Our remodel is nearly finished. Do you mind if it stays for now?"

"I don't use that room, so it's fine to leave it. But my lease expires in July, so we should talk before then in case I decide to move."

"Here they are." Jackie returned to the living room and opened a box a little larger than a deck of playing cards.

"Tarot?" I asked, curious. I hadn't known Jackie read tarot.

"Yeah. I stumbled on it when I first moved out to California. Everyone seemed very into getting readings at the time. Maybe it *was* just a fad back then, but I found I really liked it. As if the cards spoke to me in some way. A neighbor left me her old deck when she moved, so that's how I got these." Jackie shuffled the cards, her unfocused gaze fixed on the carpet.

"So how do you do a reading then?" I leaned forward with interest.

"There's a lot to Tarot. I could wax on about the history and symbology, but some of it is really quite simple. Me, I run with the first feeling or image I see in the card, allowing the reading to unfold as it will. Today I'll do a short four-card reading to answer a specific question I have in mind. In this case, whether to go to Vail."

Cutting the cards into three piles, she assembled the deck in a different order, then placed four cards face down. Jackie explained the four cards represented the past, present, challenge, and outcome, each read in order, left to right.

The first card she turned was the King of Wands wearing a fiery red cloak. Jackie's past as it related to her current question. A vivacious and energetic king, a passionate man, a magnanimous father. Definitely the Carl my cousin had fallen in love with so completely.

Her present situation was depicted by the Four of Wands, a man and woman dancing together in a pavilion. Romance, an engagement, a celebration of home. Jackie's life in the beautiful Spanish ranch house Carl bought for the two of them in one of those picturesque canyons in the Santa Cruz mountains.

The challenge card was represented by the Page of Cups, a young lady standing by the seashore holding a glowing cup out of which a fish stood on his tail peering at her. Tapping the card with one manicured fingernail, Jackie shook her head. "This card almost always means good news, or a young woman. Sometimes a pregnancy. But today this card reminds me of Carl's daughters. They are actually wonderful kids most of the time, but quite energetic and demanding of his attention. When they visit, I hear a perpetual chorus of "Daddy look at me." Both he and I end up exhausted by the girl's unceasing intensity. I know it's just kids being kids, but they are *definitely* a challenge. And they do present the complication in this situation for sure."

The outcome card was the Nine of Wands reversed, a man standing behind a fence of wands, leaning on a staff. "This is the dig in and wait and see card," Jackie said. "Delays and obstacles. Adversity. Sometimes, with the reverse interpretation, a dead end. I know that sounds terrible, but it's really been the story of my life with Carl. We've been waiting for the lawyers to settle things with the divorce and it is just taking so damn long, we get frustrated. This card tells me the

261

outcome is still stalled. Nothing is going to change. In fact, things may be delayed further. No surprise there. It is what it is. Might as well accept it."

Sighing, Jackie gathered up the cards, looking at each one in turn. "So when I think about the question of whether I should go to Vail, this outcome points to the possibility of travel delays, and more frustration on top of the current frustration. As lovely as a skiing trip sounded earlier, I don't know whether that's what I should be doing. Going home and enjoying the peace and quiet, or perhaps catching up on my design work for Carl's executive placement agency feels like a better use of my time. He'll be delighted to come home to a new set of logos and letterhead designs to jump start his creative process."

My cousin shrugged and smiled. "Now that that's settled, let's read you," she suggested. "Think about your question while I shuffle."

"I don't know, Jacks." I shifted uncomfortably on the couch. "I essentially just told Dave to take a flying leap. I don't know there's anything to read."

Jackie's face took on a thoughtful expression. Pursing her burgundy lips, she nodded. "Last night you mentioned that blonde, Candy, had been Dave's old girlfriend, but he'd been the one to break it off, right? I know you saw what you saw... but what if there's something else you need to know. A bigger picture. This is actually one of my favorite types of readings. In this case, the question would be something like... 'what do I most need to know about this relationship thing with Dave?' Wanna give it a try?"

As I watched Jackie shuffle, I decided why not. The Tarot was just a deck of cards, nothing mysterious or dangerous about that. When my cousin read the images for her own reading, I had easily followed her intuitive thinking. Frankly I'd been astounded at the accuracy of the cards she turned. I don't know whether Jacks could have ordered them up that way, even if she tried.

"Ready?"

Taking a deep breath, I nodded. "Ready."

Jackie turned the first card, the Five of Swords, a man laughing as he walks away from a fight with two other swordsmen. "Shitfire, girlfriend, no messing around here. I call this card the humiliation card. In this case, a past defeat that involved some shady tactics. A failure where nobody wins. This card is the past, but I don't know whether it is yours or his. Maybe both."

The second card was the Magician, a mystical man with the tools of his trade displayed on a table before him. "This card represents intention. Imagination. Will combined with skill. Competence. Confidence. Again, whether we're reading him or you Reets, this is a very strong card. Let's see if the other cards makes thing any clearer."

Turning the Seven of Pentacles, Jackie furrowed her brow. The card showed a youngish man in a garden surrounded by golden pentacle blossoms, the fruit of his labor.

"Wealth is the challenge?" I asked.

"It's more than that," my cousin said. "It is waiting for investments to mature, or your work to bear fruit, which requires time and patience. I think patience is the challenge here. Sometimes the wine has to mature to develop that rich taste we so love. Make sense?"

"I wonder if this reading is about Dave and me, but *separately*," I said, "as if we are on parallel paths in some way."

"Could be," Jackie said, turning the outcome card.

Both of us stared at the unpleasant image of two paupers in the snow outside a lovely stained glass church window. The window contained five pentacles gleaming in warm red and green and gold hues. "This is the 'left out in the cold' card. It can pertain to financial failure, or loss of a lover. Often it signifies homelessness — either literal or figurative. Once I saw this card interpreted as the catch 22 of a Catholic marriage, where fealty comes at all costs — including your own personal happiness. But beyond that, it's alienation, feeling cast out. Alone." Jackie looked up at me. "I'm having trouble with putting this reading together, Reets. What do you think?"

Clearing my throat, I wiped my eyes on a battered napkin I'd stuffed into the cuff of my orchid cashmere sweater. "You do realize this card is pretty damn close to where I stood last night looking in the window of Dave's cabin at his Christmas lights?"

My cousin's face blanched at the reminder, her hand reaching across the couch to touch mine. "Oh God, Reets. I didn't think. I'm so sorry."

"No. Don't be." I shook my head, tapping the first card, the Five of Swords. "The humiliation card...I definitely relate to that. Been there, done that. In spades. And apparently I haven't progressed a whole lot because I'm doing another version of it with this alienation card. Fuck."

Shaking my head, I looked at the image of the Magician, trying to put together the message. "But this Magician and the patience card sound like a different story, don't they?"

Jackie pursed her lips. "Could be, but it usually doesn't work that way. I think this is a story about *someone,*" her voice emphasized the word someone so I knew it was perhaps not only me, "who had a messy humiliating love affair in the past, but is coming into his or her own, as represented by the Magician. That someone is experiencing the challenge of waiting until the time is right to grab the success — or the love — they've waited for and worked hard to manifest. The current outcome... I think this means if they fail the challenge it could very likely make them feel alone, left out in the cold. An island so to speak." My cousin paused, and then continued. "The question we asked for this reading was 'what do I most need to know about this relationship thing with Dave,' right? I'm guessing the cards are telling you more about your dynamic, but as you said earlier, your lives may be running in parallel and the story is both of yours. The thing to remember — and this is important, Reets —the outcome is reading the current trajectory of events. All that can change if we somehow decide to make different choices."

A loud pounding on the door startled both of us. "Rita?" said a man's voice.

"What the hell?" said Jackie, gathering up the Tarot cards.

"It's Dave," I said, my hands suddenly shaking. "Oh God. I don't want to see him, Jacks. I didn't think he'd come here. Shit. What am I gonna say?"

"You're gonna go in the bedroom and let me handle it," said my cousin, shoving me gently in the back. She swished her hand in the air as if I were an errant puppy. "Go. "

As I closed the bedroom door, I heard Jackie unlock the deadbolt. I stood with my ear against the crack, hoping to hear whatever was said. I felt like a chicken-shit hiding out, but I knew I couldn't face Dave without spewing tears and a good dose of fireball histrionics. Not pretty. And probably not worth it. So why bother? I could feel the dam ready to burst in my chest just standing there in the semi-darkness. Given the last crying scene I'd had with a man when Gabe broke things off, I vowed never to do it again.

"Rita, what the hell... Oh, sorry ma'am, you're not Rita. I must have the wrong apartment."

"No. Right apartment. I'm Rita's cousin Jackie. And you are...?" Jackie kept her voice cool and detached, a woman in charge.

"Dave Higgins. I'm um... Rita's friend. Maybe she's told you about me?"

Jackie stifled a laugh. "Yeah. I know the name, Mr. Higgins. I also know a two-faced cheat when I see one. You're not welcome here. So I advise you to get the fuck off my porch before I call the cops."

"Whoa. Just a second there. I don't know what you're talking about ma'am, but you apparently have me mixed up with someone else." Dave sounded shocked.

"No I don't think so," Jackie laughed. "After your little interlude last night with your old lover a Miss Candycane, Rita doesn't care to see you anymore. I think she told you that already? So please, pursue your affections with this other woman and leave my cousin alone."

"What the hell did Candy tell her?" Dave sputtered.

"Nothin' you need to be concerned about, Mr. Higgins. Now please leave."

"Nothing happened, Rita. I swear it. Whatever she told you was a lie." Dave raised his voice so the entire apartment complex could hear him. "Please, let me explain."

"Don't give me a reason to call the law, Mr. Higgins. I have the phone in my hand."

"God damn it, Rita. Talk to me." Dave shouted.

I heard Jackie dial the phone, three short beeps, then her soft voice, all business. "Yes, I'm calling to report an attempted break-in at 1243 Sunshine Avenue..."

"All right. I'll go. I don't want any trouble. I'll go. " Dave announced. "But this ain't over, Rita. Not by a long shot."

The sound of screeching tires followed shortly. I heard Jackie shut the front door and slide the deadbolt into place. "I don't think he'll be back, Reets." The fake call had prompted Dave to leave, which was all she wanted.

Opening the bedroom door, I stumbled into my cousin's open arms. "Jacks, I'm just so...." The dam in my chest broke and I began sobbing, the hurt unbearable. "I can't believe this is happening to me again..." I cried on my cousin's shoulder like a heartbroken child.

Jackie simply held me, smoothed my curls, told me everything would be all right. I didn't believe her, but it didn't matter. We both knew the gig. Time heals all — or at a minimum takes away some of the hurt. Eventually I'd look back on my affair with Dave without the memory ripping my heart out of my chest.

If I had any heart left, that is.

Chapter Nine

Christmas night Jackie tucked me into bed with a cup of chamomile tea and a good book. Although I slept most of the following day, that next evening I headed out to Goat Rock Beach. Bundled in blankets and my flannel lined raincoat, I sat with my back against my old rock seat and watched the starry night. The sound of the ocean lulled me into a fragmented sleep and I found myself back in Glen Ellen peering into Dave's cabin window again, except this time all I saw was Dave by himself — except for Duke at his heels.

Cackling gulls startled me awake a few hours later, along with the slamming car doors of other beach visitors. The darkness had faded to a gray cloudy morning. I watched the harbor seals swim out to sea, their barking calls barely discernible over the whistling December wind, then I staggered back to my car, drove home, crawled into bed, and slept the rest of the day.

Unable and unwilling to face the world, I pled a bad cold and took the entire holiday week off. Guy Salvatore wasn't too happy about it, but I knew he'd cut me some slack because he owed me a shitload of comp time. I simply didn't want to see anyone or do anything. I plunged myself into a seven-book fantasy series, reading and sleeping, then reading some more. I called Jess and told her why I wasn't coming in to work so she wouldn't worry about me too much, then unplugged my phone to avoid talking to anyone else. Somehow I had the good sense not to drink myself sick every night.

When I returned to Sonoma Diesel after New Year's, I found a card on my desk. Thinking it was a wayward Christmas greeting, I opened it only to find it was a note from Dave. I dragged myself into the relative safety of a bathroom stall and read it against my better judgment.

Dearest Rita,

I don't know exactly what happened over Christmas, but after talking with your cousin I get that you don't want to see me and that it has something to do with Candy.

It would be better if we could talk in person, but I'm going to be away on business for the next month in Alaska, so that's not possible. The phone would definitely be a little better than a letter, but you haven't been answering... so I'm giving this writing thing a try.

Please let me explain. Candy did come over to my place Christmas Eve. I don't know what she told you, but nothing happened. I won't lie to you. She was looking to spend Christmas Eve with me the way we used to as lovers. When I told her I wasn't interested and the reason was you, she tried to initiate her old persuasive ways.

Darling... please believe me. <u>Nothing happened</u>. Not that she didn't try. But I set her gently aside, bundled her back into her coat and sent her home. That's it. End of story.

If she told you something other than that, I'll get to the bottom of it and you'll have an apology from her. I won't stand for her lying to you, or anyone else I care about ever again. Her lies nearly destroyed my best friend, not to mention contributed to the end of my first marriage. Not that I wasn't to blame as well. I admit it. But Jay... that man deserved better, and I think he's finally found it with your friend Jess.

As for me, I'm older and wiser now, and I know what I want. You're one in a million, Rita Garcia. And I want you in my life. My offer to move in still stands, if you'll have me.

I'll be flying home February 10th if all goes to plan. If you would allow me to take you to dinner on Valentine's Day, it would be my distinct pleasure.

Love, Dave

Fucking idiot man! Why would he think I wanted to read his stupid drivel? Why should I care? I crumpled the note into a ball and threw it into the toilet in frustration, then promptly fished it out, smoothed it flat again, and mopped it with paper towels. Tears streamed mascara down my cheeks in rivulets.

Where the hell did Dave get off writing such bullshit? As if I hadn't seen them kissing with my own eyes?

Moreover, why did I want to believe him?

Gazing at myself in my bathroom mirror, I applied the ruby red lipstick and blotted my lips. The color matched my brushed Chinese silk dress perfectly. I studied my image in the glass, my dark pupils holding eye contact with my reflection as if to look inside my own soul. I felt strong for a change. Unapologetically myself and unwilling to accept white lies or lame excuses from anyone, including — no especially — from someone I loved. I deserved better.

I'd give Dave a piece of my mind and be done with it.

Admittedly, I was nervous. Long-tailed cat by a rocking chair nervous. I hadn't seen Dave since the Christmas debacle, and part of me had vacillated over meeting him for dinner on Valentine's Day —as if it were some romantic date. Why go over the entire bleeding thing again? But the gold card on the red roses he'd had delivered to my office at Sonoma Diesel that morning confirmed the Valentine's dinner date he proposed in January, and although I could have called and cancelled and stuck to my old "fuck you asshole" shtick, I didn't.

I decided to give him the opportunity to explain. Not that it would make a goddamn bit of difference. But I wanted to hear what he had to say and I wanted to set the record straight: Candy hadn't said shit to me about that night. I saw the two of them together myself. No denying that.

Fucker broke my heart. And dammit I wanted to know why.

When I walked into Vicente's Bistro, I noticed Dave immediately at the bar. Those thick shoulders were easy to pick out of any crowd. He turned toward the door at that moment, as if he sensed my presence, and I saw his eyes widen in a way that told me I looked pretty damn good for a heartbroken wreck. After the maitre de seated us, we traded niceties — stilted smiling phrases you mutter when you're nervous as hell and waiting for a sip of wine to take the edge off. I could feel the floor vibrating where he unconsciously jiggled his leg up and down beneath the table.

Taking a deep breath, I opened the main topic of conversation. No sense pussyfooting around. "You invited me here tonight because...." I let the sentence dangle and looked up at him through my dark eyelashes.

"Because I was hungry for Veal Parmegana." Dave smiled, his cheeks flushing.

Deciding to play along for the moment, I smiled back. "So what else is good here?"

"Everything. Lasagna. Manicotti. Fettucini Alfredo. But I think the Veal Parmegana is the absolute best."

The waiter poured our wine with a flourish, took our order, and silently padded away. Grasping our glasses, we both spoke together, the words mingling.

"Cheers," I said, keeping it casual.

"To us," he proposed, his eyes suddenly serious. He clinked his crystal long-stemmed glass against mine, his face determined. As he took a sip, I set my glass carefully down, readying myself for the come-to-Jesus meeting I knew we needed. Time to end this charade once and for all.

"There is no us, Dave," I said softly.

"I ain't buyin' that, Rita." He shook his head, lips pressed together. "So I guess we better get to it and thrash this thing through, because I ain't leaving here until we do. You gonna go first, or should I?"

"Your note said you wanted a chance to explain. The floor is yours. I'm listening." I leaned back in my chair.   In my own way, I was handing Dave a coiled rope: either he'd pull himself out of the quagmire or sink.

Plunging in without hesitation, Dave made his points. "I ask you to move in with me. We plan to spend Christmas together. I cook prime rib for dinner, put up Christmas lights, buy champagne. And then you never show up. When I phone the next day, you tell me good-bye and good riddance and hang up on me. I go to your house to figure out what the fuck. But your cousin kicks me out and says something about my "interlude" with a Miss Candycane. I can be slow, Rita, but I'm not stupid. I get the picture: Candy called you and talked some lying shit about her and me and you're dumping me." Dave looked away, his muscled jaw set tight.

"Pissed me off," he growled, his intense sentiment palpable.

I kept my mouth shut and waited, twirling the wine glass stem between my finger and thumb and watching the golden liquid swirl around the crystal globe. So he was pissed off? Good. I was pissed off too.   But undoubtedly for an entirely different reason.

The subdued restaurant lighting cast his face into shadows. I wondered briefly whether he'd continue, but he managed to push his anger aside and speak calmly.

"I spent the last six weeks in Alaska for Nowalk. But when I got home a few days back, I had a conversation with Candy. Asked her what the hell she thought she was doing talking crap to you. 'Cept she swore she had no idea what I was talkin' about. So either she's lying — which I wouldn't put past her — or there's something more to the story. Because like I said in my note, nothing happened between Candy and me that should come between me and you." Dave studied my face, his eyes narrowing as his forehead wrinkled.

"I'm confused, Rita. One day, you're about to move in with me. The next, you're slamming the door in my face." He threw his hands up in the air in frustration, his voice rising slightly over the restaurant's low hum. "I want to know if she's spun some story to you so we can move past the bullshit and the lies and get back to us. You and me. Together."

In the silence that followed Dave's statement, the waiter delivered our dinner plates and filled our wine glasses, all formal polish and politeness. Mozzarella cheese bubbled atop the breaded cutlets, accompanied by the smell of spicy marinara. My stomach grumbled loudly, which might have been embarrassing, but in the moment provided a levity both Dave and I needed. Picking up his silverware, he sampled the fare and motioned for me to do the same.

"Best in the valley," he promised. "You'll love it."

I followed suit, letting the tender veal smothered in marinara and cheese melt in my mouth as I considered Dave's story. That he'd made the effort to confront Candy over her supposedly spilling some kettle of beans to me was mildly interesting — if it were true. But it still didn't change what I'd seen.

"Candy's not lying. About that anyway," I began. My plan was to stick to the stark facts. Say what I'd seen and be done with it. "She never called me or said anything to me about you, but I think you gave her the idea to call and confront Jess about Jay. Anyway..." I paused to twirl some spaghetti onto my fork. "Candy didn't need to tell me anything. I was there, Dave. At your house that night. Telling me nothing happened is not exactly...." I shrugged, keeping my eyes on my plate. "I saw you guys kissing through the window. That pretty much told me everything I needed to know. So, I left...."

Feeling the tears well in my eyes only made me angry. I had wanted to be able to do this without crying, damn it. I'd thought I could do it — be cold and clinical and just say my piece. Except, I couldn't. I still cared about him too much.

"Excuse me." I forced the raspy words through a throat rapidly swelling with emotion. Then I threw my napkin down and stormed from the table.

"Rita. Please. Wait." Dave's calloused hand brushed against mine, but I shook it away. I would not cry over him in a public restaurant. No fucking way.

Vicente's white tile bathroom turned out to be rather nice. Comfortable even. The bronze fixtures and slatted wooden stall doors gave the place a homey look. I leaned against the wall beneath the No Smoking sign and lit a cigarette, figuring a few quick drags wouldn't set the smoke alarm off. Hopefully no one would catch me flaunting the rules.

I barely heard the gentle knock on the door, but Dave's low voice was unmistakable. He didn't ask if I was OK, or demand I come out.

"I know you're in there, Rita. I just want to say one more thing. That night you missed the part where I turned Candy down flat. You didn't see me walk her out to the truck and insist she leave. You didn't hear me tell her I was in love with you. Because I am. I'm so in love with you I can barely see straight. I wish you would have stayed to see her leave, babe. I wish..."

Dave cleared his throat. "Uh... well, there's a lady out here with me now. I think she wants to use the restroom and I'm standin' in her way. So I'm headin' for the bar. I hope you decide to join me, but if you don't, I won't bother you anymore."

When the restroom door swung open, I had already thrown my cigarette into the toilet and flushed it away and was patting my eyes with cool water. An elderly woman with carrot orange hair and thick eyeglasses glanced at me, our eyes meeting briefly in the mirror before she entered the stall and began to go about her business.

"That young man seemed quite sincere, honey," the woman said in her quavering soprano. "You know, we all do foolish things sometimes. Make mistakes. Fall on our noses. But nothing mends a heart like an apology... and I think that's what he was trying to do. I hope you decide to give him another chance."

As the woman fell silent, I vacillated between asking her to mind her own business (telling an old lady to fuck off seemed somehow *wrong*), or pretending I hadn't heard a word she said, or simply acknowledging her wisdom. Some days it was easy for me to choose the appropriate response.

"I will... give him another chance, that is," I said, realizing I meant it. "Thank you."

"Good luck," she said, and mumbled something more, but I didn't hang around long enough to listen.

I found Dave at the end of Vicente's bar, two shots of tequila rimmed with salt in front of him, a small bowl with lime wedges ready for action. He smiled as I slipped into the seat beside him.

"You game?" he pointed to the glasses.

"You bet," I said, curling my ruby red fingertips around one of the cut crystal shot glasses.

"Have I ever told you how fabulous you look in red?" he asked, clenching the tiny glass between his thick thumb and forefinger.

"I don't believe you have," I said, raising my drink.

"To us," he said, raising his eyebrows.

"To us," I nodded, touching my glass to his. I swigged the shot down in two gulps, then sucked the lime wedge Dave placed against my lips, then kissed the persistent salty lips that immediately followed the lime. I melted into his familiar embrace, my heart dancing in my chest. Before I knew it, his fingers casually found their way under my dress and up my thigh, the dark oak bar easily hiding any trace of impropriety from the other patron's eyes.

I could have stopped him, but I didn't.

"Any chance you might let me tow you away for tea tonight, Ms. Meter?" he teased between kisses.

"If you don't tow me away soon, Mr. Higgins, my legs are going to..."

"Say no more, lovely Rita." He lifted me easily off the stool. "I have plans for you, my lady."

Chapter Ten

The following morning Dave and I rose at 5am and drove out to Goat Rock. We walked the beach together hand in hand despite the cold wind and drizzling rain. The seals barked their morning greetings as they rode the surf out to sea. I'd wanted to show him the place where I'd found such solace and healing so when he thought of me at the ocean he could really see it in his mind's eye. Because in a few days he was leaving again for Alaska.

Edgar Nowalk had purchased equipment from a failing Alaska freight company for a pittance, and asked Dave to open a satellite office in Anchorage. Dave had been away helping Nowalk assemble the truck fleet, finalize contracts, and get the shop up and running, as well as hire a crew. It was the opportunity of a lifetime and he absolutely couldn't turn it down. It was a chance to get in on the ground floor of something that could be big and see it through. A chance to build a trucking business. Like he always wanted. I was happy for him, albeit deeply sad he was leaving.

Not that he didn't ask me to go with him. He did. In the sincerest way imaginable. But I knew it wasn't the right decision. At least not right then. For either one of us.

Dave would be so busy with the business start-up, he wouldn't have time for a live-in girlfriend. And I knew that would be difficult for me because I'd never been too good at delayed gratification. I didn't have the words to explain how I knew going with him would destroy what we had. I'm not sure I understood it myself. But I did not want to ruin us by applying relationship pressure at the same time he was trying to build a business. I didn't want us to lose each other because we tried to push things too quickly too soon. As my cousin Jacks had explained in the tarot card reading, "let the wine mature."

The convoluted logic of all that didn't do a damn thing for my aching heart. Knowing something is the right decision and feeling it are two very different things. After the time Dave and I had spent together, I knew deep in my gut we had something real. Something neither one of us had ever experienced before in a relationship. Something beyond precious that many folks never have the luck to find in their entire lifetime. I couldn't stand the thought of him going, but as much as it hurt, I understood.

"I'm not saying good-bye," he told me when I dropped him at the airport.

"Me either," I said, holding on to the hope I didn't need to. Tears threatened to overwhelm my goodbye smile, but I smiled anyway. We agreed to a long distance relationship. At the time we thought we were strong enough to weather the separation. Absence makes the heart grow fonder, right?

I guess it sort of worked. For a few years. Except then life — and death —got in the way.

Don't they always?

Life arrived in the form of my cousin Jackie's daughter, Jenna, who began living with me shortly after she turned two. I'd brought her home to Santa Rosa in the wake of the automobile accident that killed my cousin Jacks and her husband Carl a mile from their home in the Santa Cruz Mountains. They'd been on the way to Carl's San Jose office together one morning. The drunk driver who snuffed out their lives stumbled away without a scratch.

Devastated by the loss of a woman I loved like a sister, I was doubly shocked to discover Jackie and Carl had named me Jenna's guardian. When the lawyer unveiled the will, it was all clear in black and white, so Jenna and I became a couple. I did it for Jacks of course, although I don't know what possessed my cousin to think of me as maternal in any fashion. At the time I simply put one foot in front of the other and embraced Jackie's sweet child as my own. Thankfully Jess's little daughter Kyna was about the same age and I had a girlfriend's shoulder to lean on as a clueless single parent.

Somehow Jenna and I got through the first few rough months and settled into a routine I grew to cherish. Seeing the simple things in life through the eyes of a child brought me more joy than I ever imagined. Which was a good thing because, I could have never prepared myself for the next curve ball life threw at me.

Death swooped in again, felling my boss Guy Salvatore with a fatal heart attack a few years later. Dropped him like a stone on his way to the coffee pot one morning. Dead before the paramedics got there a mere fifteen minutes after I frantically 911'd him. Earl Wyse, the Service Manager who served as a volunteer firefighter, issued CPR with my help, but Guy had already flown the coop. It happened so fast, I couldn't believe it. Five minutes earlier the man had been teasing me about my purple lipstick. Then he was simply gone.

A week after the funeral, Sonoma Diesel introduced the new Parts Department Manager. I sat quietly at the back of the lunchroom as the CEO delivered the news at a company meeting. They'd thought long and hard about Guy's replacement. Not that the man could ever truly be replaced; there weren't a lot of characters like old Guy. But they had chosen the candidate they thought was the best qualified for the job. Someone who had worked in heavy equipment for almost a decade and knew the Parts operation inside and out. As the announcement drew near, I closed my eyes for a moment, steeling myself to weather whatever came next.

Because the new Parts Department Manager was me.

Unexpectedly, the company staff responded with a rousing cheer. As I made my way to the podium to express my thanks, I found my hands shaking with nerves. Although Jess had long since left the company to finish school, I found myself wishing she were there in the worst way. Somehow I made it through the acceptance speech without embarrassing myself. All I remember was people laughing when I told a few stories about Guy. Obviously I could never be him — who could? — but I was honored to have the opportunity to lead the Parts team. And I'd depend on everyone at Sonoma Diesel to lend a hand.

That afternoon I left work early and took Jenna out to Goat Rock. She chased a few sandpipers, threw some stones into the water, got her sneakers soaking wet, and started digging a hole to China, while I gazed out across the roiling Pacific. Gray clouds scurried across the sky promising rain, but neither of us minded the blustery wind terribly much. The brisk breeze cleared the cobwebs out of my head the way it always had. It was really pretty simple: I'd either fall on my nose at Sonoma

Diesel and they'd put me back in my old position and hire someone else, or I'd figure it out and make Guy proud.

I won't say the next few months were a walk in the park, but I found my stride and didn't screw it up. In fact, I wasn't a month into the gig before I realized old Guy had been grooming me to take over for years, the sweet, fat knucklehead.

About six months after my promotion, I found a card on my desk postmarked Alaska. As I expected, once Dave moved up to Anchorage he'd been consumed by Nowalk's business startup and hadn't had a lot of time to maintain a long-distance relationship. As for me, becoming an instant mom to an adventurous daughter had taken nearly all my time, and energy. Single-parenting, along with moving into a management position, was enough for any 30-something, no matter how vivacious.

Dave and I hadn't actually seen each other in almost four years — since before Jacks died. Our relationship hadn't formally ended; it had simply fizzled without either of us making the time to revive it in any fashion. I was mad at him for a while for ignoring me. But eventually I'd taken the hint and dated occasionally when Jess volunteered to keep Jenna for the night. Knowing Dave the way I did, I imagined he'd been seeing others as well. Regardless, the man was a damn fond memory. I thought about him often, but never mustered the guts to take the initiative and make contact. It'd be just my luck he'd be happily married or something.

I opened the colorful card and recognized his scrawling script, remembering another note he'd written long ago that had been the first step to straightening out a horrid misunderstanding and rescued our relationship from the toilet where I'd miserably thrown it. Smiling, I read his message.

Dearest Rita,

I know it's been a while since we last talked, but I wanted to send you congratulations on your promotion. I'm proud of you. Sonoma Diesel is lucky to have you.

Things here are good. Business is booming. Our contracts up on the North Slope keep expanding. Opened a shop in Fairbanks last year too.

Anyway, I'm going to take a chance here and say what's on my mind. I miss you darling... That's my story and I'm sticking to it. Not that I've been some celibate saint over the past few years, but nobody gets me like you do. Nobody ever has.

I heard you adopted your cousin's daughter. I look forward to meeting her one day. If you ever get a hankering for an old friend, I want you to know my offer still stands. And if all we can be is friends because there's someone else special in your life now, that's OK by me.

I'll be flying down to the Bay Area in September for Nowalk's investor meetings. If you would allow me to take you to dinner one night while I'm in town, it would once again be my distinct pleasure.

Dave

I set the card on the edge of my desk where I could see the artwork, a series of stylized harbor seals, reminiscent of the animals who had graciously shared Goat Rock Beach with me for so long. For Dave to say *"my offer still stands"* thumped me in the chest like a fastball. If the last few years had taught me anything, it was life was way too short. Could I really afford to turn aside a man I cared so deeply about because he lived in Alaska?

September was three months away. There was an entire summer yet to be planned. Perhaps it was time to take Jenna on a vacation.

Chapter Eleven

"Mommy, can we go see the polar bear again today? Please?" Jenna pulled on my hand as we walked through the Captain Cook Hotel lobby, her brown curls bobbing.

"Not today, honey. But we can go back tomorrow for a quick visit." I smiled at my six year-old daughter's enthusiasm for sight-seeing. She'd loved our hiking trip to Portage Glacier, but the visit to the Anchorage Zoo the previous day had left her enamored with polar bears. She'd barely talked about anything else since.

"Can we take another boat ride and watch the seals swimming in the sea?" She flashed me an impish smile. Our trip to Seward on a whale watching excursion had been filled with the sight of seals, seals, and more seals amidst a series of rain squalls. The inclement weather had driven most of the tourists huddling inside the boat cabin for dry warmth, but Jenna and I had remained outdoors with our hoods tied beneath our chins laughing in the blustery salt wind and singing a few of her favorite songs to the cute creatures.

"Who's afraid of a little rain?" I teased.

"Not us, by golly, by gum!" she squealed, skipping beside me, her colorful rainbow cardigan flapping against her bubble-shaped rear end.

"Today we are going to pay a surprise visit to my friend Dave, remember? It's just a little walk from here. You ready?"

"Yup," she nodded, clutching her book bag. "And then we're going out for hamburgers," she reminded me, her small face serious.

A few blocks from the Captain Cook, the ARCO building loomed high into the Anchorage skyline. After riding the elevator to the 15th floor, I located Nowalk Transportation's executive office suite and entered the reception area, towing Jenna by the hand. The decor was mostly dark gleaming wood, with leather chairs and Alaskan art on the walls. In one corner, a stuffed caribou head surveyed the room with liquid chocolate eyes; on the opposite wall, floor to ceiling windows offered a view of the Chugach Mountains. Seating my daughter in the corner of one oversize leather sofa with a book on her lap, I approached the receptionist's desk. A pretty blonde woman greeted me, her curious gaze fixed on Jenna.

"Can I help you ma'am?"

"Yes. Is Mr. Higgins in?" I handed her my Sonoma Diesel business card and smiled. I'd dressed in stylish business attire, a hip length herring bone jacket over a short black pencil skirt and black silk blouse.

"My apologies, I don't see you in the appointment book, Ms. Garcia. Mr. Higgins does not take unscheduled solicitations. I'm sure you understand." The blonde flashed a professional detached smile. Doing her job meant screening Dave's visitors. Nothing short of expected. But describing my presence as a solicitation subtly painted me in a lowly light I didn't appreciate. I wondered if I was reading more into the younger woman's words than she intended, but when she gazed up at me, I could see she definitely meant the slight. Strange.

Deciding to respond graciously despite the veiled insult, I returned her smile and noted the name plate on her desk. "I do understand, Kelly. But I think Mr. Higgins will see me, regardless of whether I have an appointment. Please feel free to phone him and ask."

The woman pursed her pink lips and nearly rolled her eyes. Without bothering to check the schedule further or pick up the phone, she stood, towering over me, and spoke with a sweet civilized veneer that failed to hide her condescending tone. "Mr. Higgins is in a meeting right now, Ms. Garcia. I'll check with him over the lunch hour and if he agrees to put you on his calendar, I'll have an answer for you, say around 2PM. You may phone me to confirm, but I think the earliest he could see you is next week." She handed me a business card of her own and nodded a dismissal. "Have a nice day, Ms. Garcia. And, if we do happen to see you again, please drop your child at a daycare facility before your appointment. We do not provide babysitting services here." She smiled her cold professional smile, and returned to her paperwork.

Granted, the gal had no idea who I was, but discharging me in such a manner and suggesting I drop my daughter off with strangers like a set of baggage rankled me to the core. I took a deep breath before saying something I'd undoubtedly regret. Dave's receptionist had me uncomfortably stalled, unsure what action to take next. I could leave a hand-written note, but there was no guarantee when Kelly would pass it on. Considering my rather limited options, I returned to Jenna's sofa, picked up her book bag, and sat beside her.

From an adjacent hallway, I heard the sound of men's distinctly Southern accents coming our way. If I'd been by myself, I'd have given Miss Kelly a piece of my mind without caring who heard me. But I didn't want to create a hoo-ha with my daughter watching; it would only upset her.

"Time to go, honey," I said, trying to hide my disappointment. With only two more days in town before our return flight, an appointment the following week would mean I'd miss seeing Dave entirely. Unless Kelly actually did what she said she was going to do and showed him my card — and then if he had time to see me. No guarantee of that without pressing my point and causing a ruckus. So much for my half-baked surprise visit idea. I really should have thought the whole thing through before showing up unannounced.

"Why are we leaving?" Jenna frowned up at me in confusion. "I thought we were going to visit your friend."

As two men exited the hallway and meandered through the elegant waiting room, all I noticed were cowboy hats and blue jeans. When they passed our seat, the older man laughed over something the younger said and clapped him affectionately on the back.

"We were, but...." I paused, censoring my words. One of my biggest parenting quandaries had been how to explain human behavior to a child who loved everyone and everything in the world. I curbed my impulse to say "the lady behind the desk is a bitch," but before I could formulate a better answer, I heard my name.

"Rita?" The younger man approached me, sky blue eyes smiling.

"Jay? How are you?" I stood and stepped briefly into Jay Green's open arms, genuinely pleased to see him. Handsome as ever, he grinned down at me, then motioned toward his companion.

"Lemme introduce my dad, Jerry. Dad, this is Rita. She's the Parts Department Manager for Sonoma Diesel where I used to work."

"Well, my goodness." The older version of Jay smiled, warmly clasping my hand. "That's quite a title for such a beautiful lady."

Containing my impulse to laugh aloud at the gentlemanly compliment, I simply nodded. "Pleased to meet you Mr. Green."

"And who is this young lady?" Jay squatted down to Jenna's eye level.

"Jenna Carmichael Martin," my daughter responded, rising to her feet and proffering her hand politely.

Shaking the small hand, Jay peered up at me. "Dave know you're here?"

"No," I shook my head, "and based on my failed negotiations this morning with his jail keeper, he's not about to any time soon." I nodded at the blonde fashion model at the desk.

"That's pure bull-pucky," said Jay, springing to his feet. "Easy enough to fix." He eyed Kelly, then leaned over to mutter in my ear. "I think she's actually part Nazi with something lodged permanently up her... you know." He waggled his eyebrows communicating his opinion, his language semi-discrete in front of my daughter. "Kelly hates me, but I don't give a rat's tutu...."

Crossing the waiting area toward the carpeted hallway where he'd recently exited, Jay raised his voice. "Dave, get your bee-hind out here, man. Somethin' you gotta see."

"Mr. Green," Kelly admonished, eyes troubled as she rounded her desk to stand in Jay's path, "please keep your voice down. Mr. Higgins is not available for any more appointments today." She looked at me pointedly.

"Stick it, Kelly," Jay said calmly, his handsome smile shining. "Dave!"

"He's on a phone call," she insisted, her sleek jaw firm. In heels, the blonde nearly topped six feet, tall enough to look Jay directly in the eye. She placed her hands on her slim hips.

"Well then I'll get him off the damn call," Jay responded, quickly pivoting around her. "Dave!" he bellowed "Get out here."

"You must be someone important, honey," Jerry Green said, his water-blue eyes appraising me.

Shrugging, I smiled politely, avoiding eye contact with Kelly, whose lips had formed an unconscious snarl. Sudden understanding bloomed in my brain, as if the woman were wearing a painted sign on her forehead that read 'hopelessly in love with my boss'. I briefly wondered whether Dave returned the sentiment when I heard his voice. The sound thrummed in my ears, the low vibration barely discernible, but I could feel it in my hips.

"Hold your horses, Jay." The words echoed down the hall. "Whatta ya got that's so all-fire important?"

"Got a surprise for you, bud." Jay turned and grinned at me, then collected his father by the elbow and propelled him double-time toward the dinging elevator doors. "Gotta go, Reets. I'll leave you to it. Bye Jenna." And with that, Jay and Jerry Green stepped into the elevator and summarily disappeared, leaving me standing in the posh waiting area wondering whether Dave's secretary would ever stop staring at me as if I smelled like a dung beetle.

"What are you talking 'bout now? I'm supposed to be on a call to...." Dave rounded the corner by the receptionist's desk and stopped in his tracks. His face registered my presence with a broad smile, his eyes crinkling at the edges. His dark blond hair held a sprinkling of silver at the temples, a sophisticated look to match his tailored wool suit jacket. Dave Higgins had never been a pretty man like his friend Jay Green, but that had never made any difference to me.

"It's you," he said, studying my eyes, then the small girl standing beside me.

Discarding business protocol, he closed the distance between us in three long steps and gathered me into his arms without hesitation. "Have I ever told you how fabulous you look in black?" he mumbled so only I could hear.

Laughing, I leaned my forehead against his shoulder, enjoying the familiar smell of mint soap and the feel of his muscles beneath the tailored jacket. "I don't believe you have, but—"

"But nothin'," he interrupted. "May I kiss you?" He pulled back to gaze down into my face. The dark green eyes were serious. His question inferred so much more than a simple kiss. He was asking if there was anyone else.

"Please do," I said, and stood on tiptoe to kiss him instead. I let the kiss linger, a signal that I was absolutely available. I didn't care one whit that Kelly was watching from behind her desk, mouth agape.

A moment later, my daughter's small voice penetrated my haze. "Mom, can we go for hamburgers now?"

"Yes, honey," I answered, stepping reluctantly out of Dave's strong arms. "But first I want you to meet my friend, Mr. Higgins. Dave, this is Jenna."

"Hamburgers for lunch?" Dave said. "My favorite, Jenna. May I join you?"

"Sure," Jenna said, staring up at Dave's formidable height. "If my mom says...."

Reaching out his huge hands, Dave grabbed my little girl around the waist an hoisted her easily up to his chest. "We can convince her, don't you think? It'll be fun. Hey, have you seen the polar bear at the Anchorage Zoo?" He raised his eyebrows at my giggling daughter as he walked toward the elevators without me. "Coming, Ms. Meter?"

I gathered my purse and Jenna's book bag, a beaming grin on my face. Being called Ms. Meter told me everything I needed to know. Dave's offer still stood; all I needed to do was accept it.

"Only if you promise to tow me away for tea later." I smiled, my return offer clear.

Dave bent forward to let Jenna poke the elevator button then turned toward me. His eyes glowed mischievously, his lips twisting into a knowing smile. "Wild horses couldn't stop me. I have plans for you, my lady."

"Do tell, Mr. Higgins," I laughed. "Do tell."

Coming Soon

Flight of the Toucan: Stories and Poems by Gianna's Granddaughters

This collection features stories and poems by cousins Emma and Lucia Martinez, Gianna's granddaughters. Selections include *Tino's Diner, Casa Del Sol, An Otter's Tale, Flight of the Toucan*, and others, in settings as diverse as North Central Washington, the Guatemalan rainforest, San Diego's Old Town, and the wilds of Alaska.

Keep reading for an excerpt.

Excerpt

Flight of the Toucan:
Stories and Poems by Gianna's
Granddaughters

The sound of buzzing insects surrounds me as I fly through the dense forest canopy. The early morning rain has washed the trees clean. Every leaf glistens. The spicy scent of ripe fruit makes my stomach growl, but there is no time to stop for a bite of breakfast. I follow the muddy trail toward Santiago Atitlan, hoping I am not too late.

My mother insisted I stay home and help with chores. "Lucia is the best with the goats," she always tells my aunties. But I know it is not the goats that drove her decision; it is my crooked foot. Instead, she sent my brother and sister, riding bicycles borrowed from Old Tito's widow with bananas laced to the handlebars and a rack on the back. I fear my teenage sister is too pretty to travel the forest trails these days without the wandering soldiers taking notice. My twin brother is only twelve. His skinny arms are still boy-sized—no match for a man intent on mischief.

I worry.

My mother worries too. She told my brother and sister to stay on the bicycles and ride fast. No stops. No swimming at the lake. Deliver the bananas to Don Carlos in the market. He will give them money to buy the medicine we need for Papa.

Ahead I see a bare branch, a good place to rest. I flex the unfamiliar green-blue feet and angle the black wings. Reaching, reaching, I clutch at the smooth mottled bark, until it moves—a boa constrictor. I quickly veer right, screams rising in my yellow throat. Leaves slap my face as I tumble through wet foliage. Spider monkeys bark and laugh as I plummet toward the ground. Flapping my tired wings, I regain control and land on an unoccupied branch. My breath is short, heartbeat aflutter.

Never have I journeyed so far in my dreaming alone. My mother thinks I'm watching the goats. She would be so angry if she knew I was asleep. But my cuarandera grandmother in San Pedro would understand. My cousin Emma far away in Wenatchee, Washington would understand too.

I had to come. Because of what I know. Because I love my family.

Bicycle tracks mark the muddy path below. A flock of scarlet macaws with bright rainbow wings whiz pass me in the opposite direction,

"Wreeeeek, wreeeek," they cry. Soldiers coming.

I must hurry.

Testing the wings again, I follow the thin trail through the forested hills. Finally I find my brother and sister. One of the bicycles has a flat tire. My brother is trying to fix it with some silver tape and an old wheezing air pump. My sister's face is frightened. She's trying not to cry.

Lighting on a nearby tree limb, I sing to catch her attention. "Arewwwww, regewww." I hop branch to branch. Anna watches me, then smiles.

"Look at that rainbow toucan, Emilio," she points. "You never see them alone." Anna's eyes are soft and kind. "Are you lost little one?"

Emilio's dark brow creases. "Funny bird. Reminds me of Lucia," he laughs, white teeth bright.

I hear the soldier's voices before my sister does. I am so scared for her. I know my brother will try to fight them, and the men will laugh at him. Emilio will blame himself for what happens, and Anna will never be her kind self again. I can't explain how I know this or why I see things that haven't happened yet. I never want to see these terrible things, but, as my grandmother told me, one cannot always choose what one sees.

About the Author

Jesse Devyn Crowe lives in the beautiful Pacific Northwest with her fisherman husband and two adventurous Labrador Retrievers. Originally born and raised in New England, Jesse had the distinct pleasure of living seven years in both California and Alaska, two great lands that left a distinct mark on her writing. The rest, as they say, is herstory — a tale of a girl who grew into a woman and a mother and a waitress and a writer and lots of other hats in between. An introvert by nature, Jesse enjoys living off the beaten path at the very edge of the grid (her preference being hot showers, not to mention electricity to power her laptop). She enjoys gardening, bird-watching, and hiking, as well as the occasional weekend gathering of wild women friends. She is currently finishing a novel series.

Acknowledgements

I owe a debt of deep gratitude to my teachers, past and present, along with the fabulous women friends in my life who lovingly hold up the mirror for me to better see myself. Although the list could go on for a few miles, there are four incredible women in particular who helped me immensely on this project...

... Elaine Sorrentino, my almost-twin cousin, who reads my drafts, even if they are half-baked, and offers wisdom extraordinaire

... Leslie Fleming, who believes in me even when I don't believe in myself

... Kathy Hamling, who has known me since I was fifteen and still likes me anyway, and whose perspective I treasure

... and Diana Bolton, who encouraged, counseled, and designed and, well, without whom this project would still be on my laptop!